MW01514263

MOCHA, MARRIAGE AND MURDER

A CHOCOLATE CENTERED COZY MYSTERY

CINDY BELL

CONTENTS

Copyright © 2021 Cindy Bell

All rights reserved.

All rights reserved. No part of this publication may be reproduced or transmitted in any form or by any means, electronic or mechanical, including photocopy, recording, or any information storage or retrieval system, without permission in writing from the publisher.

This is a work of fiction. The characters, incidents and locations portrayed in this book and the names herein are fictitious. Any similarity to or identification with the locations, names, characters or history of any person, product or entity is entirely coincidental and unintentional.

All trademarks and brands referred to in this book are for illustrative purposes only, are the property of their respective owners and not affiliated with this publication in any way. Any trademarks are being used without permission, and the publication of the trademark is not authorized by, associated with or sponsored by the trademark owner.

ISBN: 9798731482776

CHAPTER 1

"*Y*ou're humming." Charlotte Sweet nudged her granddaughter, Ally Sweet, with her elbow.

"Huh?" Ally glanced up from the tray of candies she had just finished emptying.

"You're humming." Charlotte grinned as she met her eyes.

"Oh sorry, I didn't realize." Ally blushed as she looked back down at the empty tray.

"There's nothing wrong with it." Charlotte wrapped her arm around her shoulders and squeezed. "I'm happy, to see you so happy."

"It's true." Ally laughed as she leaned her head against her grandmother's. "I'm just so excited."

"Most brides are stressed the week leading up to

their wedding, but you seem to be handling it just fine, even with Mrs. Bing, Mrs. Cale, and Mrs. White in charge of the catering." Charlotte glanced at the order sheet above the table. "We only have a few more boxes to fill."

"I'm only so relaxed because you've been so much help, Mee-Maw. Without you working in the shop with me, I don't think I would have managed to fill all of these orders, plus get everything arranged for the wedding. I'm sure they will do a great job with the catering." Ally smiled.

"I wish I had the same faith in them as you do." Charlotte shook her head. "The way they bicker, it worries me a bit. It's okay to tell them that you're going with someone else, that's all I'm saying, Ally." She pulled a tray of chocolates from the cooling area and set it down on the counter.

"I think it will be great!" Ally grinned as she lined up some empty boxes to fill. "It's so nice of them to offer. They're so excited about it. What's the worst that could happen?"

"With those three?" Charlotte raised an eyebrow. "I'll be surprised if it doesn't come to blows over where the soup bowl goes, and how many rolls to put in the basket."

"Yes, they can be a little wild, but their hearts are

always in the right place. Besides, Mrs. White will keep everyone in line." Ally began filling one of the boxes with candies.

"I'm sure she will at least try." Charlotte began filling another box. "I'm looking forward to making the cake, that's for sure. I am grateful that you are letting me do it."

"Letting you?" Ally looked at her grandmother. "Mee-Maw, I am absolutely honored that you offered. Don't tell Luke, but I'd get married to anyone just to have some of that cake." Ally smiled as she thought of her fiancé, Detective Luke Elm.

"Ally!" Laughter burst past Charlotte's smile.

"I mean, it's great that I also get to marry a wonderful man, but really, the cake is what's doing it for me." Ally grinned.

"Stop! You're so bad." Charlotte gave her a light push on the shoulder as she smiled. "I know how excited you are to spend the rest of your life with Luke."

"I don't hide it well, do I?" Ally's cheeks warmed as she dropped a candy into the box. "I know I've been married before, but this time it feels so different. I was going through the motions the first time, it felt like it was expected, but this time it's something I truly want. And to think it all came from moving back home, after I felt as if everything had fallen apart."

"It just shows that you never know what will happen in the future." Charlotte tipped her head into the side of Ally's and smiled. "I couldn't be happier for the two of you."

"I'm happy, too. But I will be happier when all of the planning is done. This last-minute running around takes away some of the fun. Sometimes, I wonder if there wasn't a simpler way of doing things. We have to go out to the venue today and give our final payment, but on the way, we're going to stop by the dress shop and the florist. Once that's done, we're pretty much ready, and can just enjoy each other's company until the weekend." Ally put the lid on the box of candies.

"Ally! The dress shop?" Charlotte frowned. "Luke can't go in there with you, what if he sees your dress?"

"Oh, Mee-Maw, I don't worry about those superstitions. But I'm sure he'll want to wait in the car. It's not exactly a thrilling way to spend the morning for him either. I just have to check out a few changes they made to the veil, it'll be a quick trip."

"You picked out such a beautiful dress." Charlotte

put the lid on the box of candies in front of her. "And the venue is gorgeous, too. When I was there last year for Paul and Mia's wedding, I was stunned by all of the little details they added in to make it special."

"Everyone loves it. I like the fact that it will be mostly outside, then we can go into the barn to eat and dance." Ally shrugged. "I'm just not so sure Luke is that thrilled with it."

"What makes you think that?" Charlotte grabbed another box to fill.

"I'm not sure exactly. He kept asking me if I was sure it was what I wanted. He even suggested getting married in a church." Ally smiled and shook her head. "I like the simplicity of it, but sometimes I wonder if he imagined something different."

"I'm sure he just wants to make sure that you have a beautiful day." Charlotte patted Ally's shoulder. "My guess is, all that matters to him, is that he gets to marry you."

"Aw, that's sweet. That, and getting a slice of that mocha cake you're making. It's so clever to include two of our favorite things, coffee and chocolate." Ally grinned. "The cake is one thing he hasn't stopped talking about."

"Good to know. I know it isn't traditional, but

hopefully it will be delicious." Charlotte filled the next box.

"Of course it will be." Ally smiled. "You make the most amazing cakes, Mee-Maw."

"Thanks, honey." Charlotte closed up the box. "Sometimes, all of the details can be overwhelming. I'm sure as the day gets closer, he will start to share in the excitement."

"I hope so. But either way, I'm just glad it's happening. With his work schedule, and Charlotte's Chocolate Heaven being so popular, I wasn't sure that we were going to make it work so soon."

Ally dropped the last candy into the last box and placed the lid on it. As she glanced up at the clock she gasped.

"Oops, I wasn't paying attention to the time. We are supposed to be on the road by now. Luke wants to walk the grounds a bit around the barn. Something about making sure there are no wild animals nearby. I think he's still getting used to living in the country." Ally laughed. "I'm not sure what he's expecting, a bear or a skunk?"

"Smart of him to consider it." Charlotte waved her toward the door. "Go on, I'll make sure these orders get picked up."

"Thank you so much, Mee-Maw!" Ally gave her a

quick hug, then headed for the front of the shop. She picked up her purse and pulled out her phone. She saw a few texts from Luke. The last one let her know he was outside. She stepped out through the front door and noticed his car.

Luke leaned casually against the side of it, his gaze cast up toward the sky. As she searched for any hint of annoyance at being kept waiting, she noticed the way the sun danced across his skin. Butterflies. The details of the wedding didn't really matter to her, all that mattered was marrying Luke.

"Sorry, I lost track of the time, Luke!" Ally started across the parking lot.

"Hey beautiful." Luke stood up from the car and walked toward her with a warm smile.

"I'm sorry, I didn't realize you were out here, I hope you weren't waiting long." Ally walked up to him and met his lips with a quick kiss.

"I wasn't. I was just about to come get you." Luke gazed into her eyes as he wrapped his arms around her. "I wish we could spend the day together relaxing, instead of running errands."

"Don't worry, we'll have some time after everything." Ally brushed her fingertips back through his hair and studied him with a smile. "I can't believe this is happening. You're sure right? There's still time to back out."

"Ally!" Luke rolled his eyes as he tightened his grip on her. "You have to stop asking me that." He kissed her forehead.

"That's not actually an answer." Ally raised an eyebrow.

Luke dropped down to one knee and looked up at her. As he took her hand and met her eyes, he smiled.

"Ally, I'll propose to you every single day for the rest of our lives, if that's what it takes to convince you that I'm sure." Luke squeezed her hand. "So, will you?"

"Stop being silly, we're going to be late." Ally laughed as she pulled him back up to his feet.

"That's not really an answer." Luke smiled.

"Every single day, I will, of course, Luke." Ally laughed.

Luke looked at his watch. "You're right, we do have to get going. I want everything to go smoothly."

"It will." Ally patted his chest. "Don't worry." She walked around to the passenger side of the car and climbed in.

Luke started the car and glanced over at her. "Where to?"

"First stop is the dress shop." Ally scrolled through the to-do list on her phone. "We're almost at the end of all of this. Just need to confirm the flower order, and then make the final payment at the venue, and we'll be ready to go. But can we quickly stop at the cottage first and check on Arnold and Peaches. It won't take long. I came to the shop early today, so I want to check on them."

"Of course." Luke smiled. "I wouldn't mind seeing Peaches, and my buddy Arnold of course."

Ally remembered how shocked Luke was that her grandmother had a pot-bellied pig as a pet. But they had quickly become friends.

Luke pulled into the driveway of the cottage and they both got out. Ally walked to the front door. As she approached, she heard meowing and squealing. They had obviously heard the car pull up.

Ally opened the door and stepped inside with Luke close behind. Arnold and Peaches ran straight over to them. The orange cat wound around her legs and Ally bent down to pet her. Arnold ran past Ally and straight to Luke.

"Hi buddy. Good to see you." Luke smiled as he crouched down to greet him.

"I'll get some food for them, if you take them out

CINDY BELL

the back for a quick run?" Ally started toward the kitchen.

"Perfect." Luke walked over to the back door.

As Ally prepared their food she heard Luke's laughter, which immediately brought a smile to her lips. She looked through the kitchen window to find Peaches hot on Arnold's tail.

Ally placed their bowls on the floor.

"Food's ready." She called out. The animals ran straight past Luke into the house.

As they ate their food she filled their water bowls.

"Okay, we better get going." She looked over at Luke and patted Arnold and Peaches goodbye. They walked straight over to their beds and lay down.

"Eating is tiring, it seems." Luke laughed, then followed Ally out to the car.

"To the dress shop first." Ally put on her seatbelt.

"Great." Luke pulled onto the street and headed in the direction of the dress shop. "You've been so busy with all of this, and running the chocolate shop, I hope you're not wearing yourself out."

"I don't mind." Ally smiled as she glanced at him. "It's for our special day. We only get to get married once. Well, twice for me, but this is the last time."

"Promise?" Luke grinned as he glanced at her, then ducked out of the way of her swat. "I'm kidding, I'm just kidding. You've done a great job with all of this. I know I haven't been much help." He shook his head. "Things at work have been pretty quiet, but that means catching up on a ton of paperwork. But the good thing is, we'll have plenty of time to relax and enjoy our honeymoon, no rush to get back to work."

"Honeymoon?" Ally blinked. "What honeymoon? I thought we agreed that we needed to get back to work the day after the wedding. The shop will be busy, and there's bound to be a few crimes that need your attention."

"Not funny, Ally." Luke turned into the parking lot of the dress shop. "You're mine, for a whole week. Nothing is changing that."

"Hm, I don't remember agreeing to that?" Ally's eyes widened as she shook her head. "I'll have to check my schedule."

"You!" Luke put the car in park.

"Oh right, that honeymoon." Ally laughed. "I guess, I could make some time for that." She popped open the door of the car.

Luke opened his door as well.

"Where are you going?" Ally caught his arm.

"We're going into the dress shop, right?" Luke frowned.

"You can't come in there." Ally's heart skipped a beat.

"Oh?" Luke laughed. "Why?"

"I want the dress to be a surprise." Ally shrugged, then smiled. "I'll be right back."

"Alright, I'll be here, picturing you in your wedding dress." Luke turned on the radio.

CHAPTER 2

*lly hurried into the dress shop.

"Ally, there you are!" Morgan greeted her with a quick hug. "I was wondering when you might show up."

"Sorry, we got a late start." Ally handed her a box of her favorite candies. She was a regular at the chocolate shop.

"Thank you." Morgan smiled as she placed the box on the counter. "Don't worry about being late, you're going to love this." She opened a small, white box and lifted out a gauzy veil. "See the beading in the lace?" She pointed out tiny white and silver beads that had been added to the veil. "I just knew it would be perfect. Do you like it?"

"It's gorgeous." Ally blushed as she looked it over. "I don't know though, maybe it's a little too fancy?"

"Ally, just try it on." Morgan helped her position it on her head, then walked her over to a mirror. "Take a look, and tell me if you want to change it."

Ally took a sharp breath as she saw her reflection in the mirror. The veil sparkled in the overhead lights, but its beauty paled in comparison to the rush of excitement she felt.

"This is really happening, isn't it? I'm really getting married to Luke."

"Yes, honey, it's happening." Morgan smiled as she lifted the veil off of Ally's head. "So, that's a yes on the veil?"

"Yes, it's perfect. Thank you." Ally took a deep breath, then cleared her throat. "Okay, on to the florist."

"Good luck! I'm sure Gloria has everything ready for you." Morgan waved to Ally as she walked out the door.

"Is it purple?" Luke started the engine as she climbed back into the car.

"Is what purple?" Ally stared at him.

"The dress? I was picturing purple. You look beautiful in purple."

"No, it's not purple!" Ally laughed. "The florist is next."

"Too bad, I love you in purple." Luke drove a few blocks down to the florist, then parked again. "Can I come in this time or are the flowers a surprise, too?"

"If you keep teasing me, I'm going to send you home!" Ally smiled.

Luke laughed. "Let's go look at some flowers, that could never be as beautiful as you."

"Cheesy Luke, real cheesy." Ally laughed as she stepped out of the car.

She pulled the door of the florist open and Luke walked in behind her.

"Ally, Luke, it's so good to see you!" Gloria set down the bouquet of flowers in her hand and walked over to them. "I don't need much of your time, just need you to go over a few of the arrangements." She led them over to a small, white table with matching chairs.

"I'm sure everything will be just fine." Ally sat down across from her.

"Let's see, let's see." Gloria flipped open an album and ran her fingertip over the pictures. "Yes, here we are. This is the bouquet you chose, right?" She looked up at Ally with a smile.

Ally stared down at the bouquet, then shook her

head. "No, we decided on yellow and white, remember?"

"Oh, that's right, so sorry. It's been quite a busy morning." Gloria flipped through the pages of the album, then pointed to another picture. "This one, right?"

"Yes, that's it. It is the one you ordered, right?" Ally looked into her eyes.

"It is, absolutely, the change just slipped my mind. It's lovely. I had a similar one at my wedding." Gloria's lips pursed, then she shook her head. "It was the only beautiful thing about that day."

Ally glanced at Luke, then looked back at Gloria. "I'm sorry to hear that." She knew that Gloria wasn't married, so she presumed the marriage hadn't worked out.

"Oh, look at me, bringing down the room." Gloria laughed as she patted the back of Ally's hand. "Don't worry about that, I'm sure your day will be much more pleasant. I did get a nice vacation out of it. It was a destination wedding." She flipped through the pages again. "And here are the arrangements for the tables, and the archway."

"Yes, perfect." Ally smiled as she took Luke's hand. "Aren't they beautiful?"

"Sure." Luke nodded as he looked at the flowers.

"Is it too late to add one more last-minute thing?" Ally winced. "I understand if it is."

"No, of course not, anything for the bride." Gloria grinned. "What would you like?"

"Maybe a splash of purple?" Ally glanced at Luke.

A smile spread across his lips as he met her eyes.

"Ah yes, that would be lovely, certainly. Just in the bouquet, or in all of the arrangements?" Gloria flipped through the pages again.

"Just the bouquet, I think." Ally nodded.

"Great, that's a simple change to make. No problem." Gloria made a few notes, then looked up at them. "I'm so looking forward to setting everything up."

"Thanks so much, Gloria." Ally walked toward the door.

"Purple was a great choice!" Gloria called out as she walked toward the counter. "It's a great color for you!"

"See?" Luke grinned as he held the door open for her.

"I see." Ally laughed. "But the dress is still not purple."

As they drove out toward the farm, Ally began to relax. Many of the last-minute details had been ironed out.

"Wow, we started out late, but these stops have been so quick, we've made up some time. We'll be a few minutes early, so we'll have some time to look for those predators you're worried about." Ally flashed him a smile.

"You'll thank me when our wedding isn't invaded by a family of skunks." Luke turned down the long, dirt road that led to the barn.

"Skunks, I knew that's what you were worried about!" Ally laughed. "That would be quite a disaster."

"Don't worry, I'll protect you." Luke smiled as he looked over at her. Then his smile faded. He sniffed the air as the car rolled down the long driveway. "Do you smell that?"

"What?" Ally sniffed as well. "Smoke." She narrowed her eyes. "Maybe they're burning leaves?"

"No." Luke's hands tightened on the steering wheel. "No, that doesn't smell like leaves." He rounded the bend of the driveway.

"Fire!" Ally gasped at the sight of flames leaping out of the roof of the barn in the distance. "The barn is on fire!"

Luke pressed down hard on the gas pedal. "I hope no one is inside, that is burning fast!"

Ally fumbled for her phone to call for help.

Luke stopped the car a safe distance from the barn, then jumped out.

"Luke! Stay back!" Ally jumped out of the car as well, with her phone pressed to her ear. "There's a fire on Castleman's farm! The barn is on fire." She ended the call as Luke started toward the barn. "No don't!" She grabbed his wrist and pulled him back. "Luke, it's too dangerous."

"Someone could be inside!" Luke frowned as he looked into her eyes. "I have to check!"

"I can't believe this!" A shout from the other side of the barn alerted them both to the presence of someone else.

Ally ran to the other side and caught sight of the owner of the farm, Blake Castleman. He stared at the barn as it burned.

"I can't believe this is happening!"

"Blake!" Luke jogged over to him. "Is there anyone inside?"

"There shouldn't be. No one was due to be here this morning. My wife is back at the house. I came down here to fix things up for your visit, but the barn was already on fire." Blake pulled off his cowboy hat and threw it on the ground. "This is it! This is going to ruin me!"

Ally patted his back in an attempt to comfort him.

"So, you're not sure if there's anyone?" Luke walked closer to the barn. "I have to check!"

"Luke, be careful please!" Ally frowned as he made his way toward the doors of the barn.

"Hello?" The crackling flames muffled Luke's shout. "Hello, is there anyone in there? Hello?"

Ally turned as she heard the siren of a firetruck. She caught sight of the red truck as it made its way down the driveway.

"Luke, the firefighters are here! Back away, the whole thing might collapse!" Ally winced as she heard a loud creak. "Luke!"

Without a second thought Ally rushed forward and grabbed his arm.

"Ally!" Luke gasped as he met her eyes, then propelled her back toward Blake just as part of the roof of the barn caved in.

Embers flew in all directions as more of the barn began to give way.

Ally's heart pounded as she sensed smoke, heat, and embers all around her.

"It's okay, we're okay." Luke held her hand. "It's going to be fine. No one is inside."

Within minutes, more of the barn collapsed, and the firefighters managed to extinguish the flames.

"It's gone." Blake shook his head as he stared at the rubble. "It's all gone. All of that work."

One of the firefighters called out from the middle of the remains of the barn.

"I've got a body!"

CHAPTER 3

"What? Craig, did you say there's a body?" Luke stepped forward. "But no one was inside! I called out to make sure!"

"Stay back for the moment." Another fireman guided Luke away from the barn.

"Who could be inside?" Blake's voice cracked as he looked in the direction of his house. "I know my wife is at home, I spoke to her before I left. There shouldn't be anyone in there!"

Craig walked toward them.

"Do you know who it is?" Blake asked.

"No, I don't recognize him as a local. It could be a squatter." Craig frowned as he pulled off his helmet. "That happens sometimes. People aren't aware that someone is sleeping in one of their outbuildings, and so we don't expect anyone to be inside."

Ally noticed another firetruck pull up to the scene. When the firefighters got out of the truck Ally recognized the fire captain, Dom. He walked over to Craig. Ally couldn't hear what they were saying, but their expressions were tense. When Dom was finished speaking to Craig he walked over to them.

"We need to see if we can identify the victim. All of you need to stay back. The barn has to be treated as a crime scene, now, right Luke? Until we prove otherwise." Dom looked over at Luke.

"Yes, absolutely. If there is a death involved, we need to investigate." Luke pulled his phone from his back pocket. "I'll get a few officers out here to help your men with the initial investigation."

"Let me see what's happening, and I'll come give you an update. Okay?" Dom put his helmet on his head.

"Yes." Luke clenched his jaw. Ally could see that he wanted to argue with him. Luke watched Dom walk into the partially collapsed building, then turned to Ally.

"I wish we could have helped." Ally looked at him.

"Me too."

"We have to help now." Ally turned away from

the still smoldering barn. "We have to find out who it was, and what happened."

"Of course, we will." Luke nodded. "We're going to get this all figured out."

Dom stepped out of the burnt structure and waved to Luke, just as the other officers began to arrive.

Luke led Ally over to him.

Blake walked over as well.

"Luckily, the whole building wasn't completely destroyed. We might never have found the body." Dom looked between them. "Whatever started this fire, made it burn incredibly strong." He eyed Blake as his voice thickened. "We're going to have to investigate the cause."

"What do you mean?" Blake took a slight step back. "Obviously it was an accident. We put electrical wiring in there for the receptions, and something must have been faulty. I've had it inspected. Everything was up to code. But something must have been wrong."

"Alright, that's a good start." Dom nodded. "Luckily, the fire was extinguished before the flames engulfed the whole barn and I was able to find some identification." He cleared his throat as he looked at

Blake. "Do you know anyone named Vincenzo Grange?"

"Vinnie?" Blake gasped as he took a step back. "Are you telling me that's Vinnie in there?"

"I believe so." Dom raised an eyebrow. "We will have to wait for the medical examiner to confirm his identity officially, however. I gather you know him. How?"

"Yes, I know him. He's the groom in a wedding party. They are due to get married tomorrow!" Blake's eyes widened as he dug in his pocket for his phone. "I can't believe this! Why would he be here? We weren't supposed to meet up until noon." He paused as he looked at his phone. "Until now, we were due to meet now." He turned as a car made its way down the driveway. "Oh no." He took a sharp breath. "That must be his bride, Becca. I can't believe this! How could this happen?"

"We arrived a little early for our appointment." Ally frowned. "Maybe he did as well, to have a look around." Her eyes settled on the car as it pulled to a stop not far from them.

"What's happened?" A woman with long, curly, brown hair stepped out of the passenger side of the car.

The driver stepped out as well, a man with the

same dark curls, peppered with silver. He surveyed the state of the barn.

"This doesn't look good."

A second woman, who appeared to be a bit older than the other woman stepped out of the rear driver's side of the car. Her hair was the same shade of brown, but cut short.

"Becca, you should definitely call Vinnie. Try and get hold of him and make sure he knows about this." She turned toward the younger woman.

"You're right, Tanya, I'll call him now." Becca began to dig in her purse for her phone.

"Becca." Ally stepped closer to her, in the same moment that Luke did.

"Do I know you?" Becca stared at Ally, then shook her head. "No, I don't think I do. Do you know what happened here?"

"I'm Detective Luke Elm with the Blue River Police Department and I'm afraid I have some terrible news for you." Luke glanced at the older man beside her, and the woman who stood a few feet away from her, then turned his attention back to Becca. "We don't have final confirmation yet, but it appears that Vinnie is dead."

"What?" Becca's shriek threatened to drown out

the sirens that continued to blare. "What are you talking about? He's dead? My Vinnie is dead?"

"I'm so sorry, Becca." Ally put her arm around her shoulders.

"Wait a minute, wait just a minute!" The man pulled Becca out of Ally's grasp and leaned her against his chest instead. "Are you telling my daughter that her fiancé was inside of that barn?"

"He hasn't been formally identified, but the man had Vinnie's wallet in his pocket. When we arrived, the barn was already on fire, sir." Luke shook his head as he glanced over at the rubble. "Do you know why he was here? Did he tell any of you that he was coming early?"

"What does that matter?" Tanya huffed. "Vinnie's dead. What does it matter why he was here? He was supposed to marry my cousin tomorrow! He probably came here to look things over." She glared at the owner who stood beside one of the police officers that had arrived.

"Did you even know that he was here?" Ally looked at Becca.

"No," Becca whispered the word as she clung to her father. "No, we didn't know."

"Please, Gus, you have to believe me. This is just a

terrible, terrible accident." Blake shook his head as he looked at the older man.

"An accident?" Tanya crossed her arms as she stared straight at Blake. "I find that hard to believe. What kind of accident would prevent a man from running out of a barn that's on fire? Why wouldn't he have called for help?"

"We're going to find out exactly what happened in that barn." Luke looked into Gus' eyes. "I will get every answer I can for you."

"You do that." Gus stared back at him. "You make sure you find out what happened." He held Becca's hand. "Come with me, darling, let's get you away from here."

Luke frowned as he watched them get back in their car, then turned and handed Ally the keys to his car.

"I'll get a ride back with one of the guys. I should stay at least until the scene is processed. Is that okay?"

"Of course." Ally kissed his cheek. "Call me later."

"I will."

Ally's heart raced as she watched Luke walk away with the phone against his ear. At the start of her day her main concern was getting Luke a bit more excited about their wedding. Now, the wedding was the furthest thing from her mind.

As Ally started the car and backed away from the remains of the barn, she was determined to help find out exactly what had happened to Vinnie and who had burned down the barn.

CHAPTER 4

*A*lly drove straight back to Charlotte's Chocolate Heaven. It wasn't the sweet smells she needed, it was her grandmother's presence. As soon as she walked through the door, Charlotte turned to face her.

"Ally, what's wrong?" Charlotte's eyes widened as Ally ran to her for a hug.

"Mee-Maw, it's terrible." Ally sighed as she felt her grandmother's arms embrace her. "When we went out to the venue, the barn was on fire. Someone died."

"What?" Charlotte gasped. "Someone was killed."

"Yes. It was the groom from a wedding that was supposed to take place tomorrow." Ally pulled away and sat down on a stool at the counter. "I just can't believe it happened. I wish I could have done something to help."

"Ally, there was nothing you could have done." Charlotte sat down beside her and patted her knee.

"No, you're right. The barn was already burning fiercely when we arrived." Ally looked at her grandmother.

"Do you know who the victim is?" Charlotte asked.

"Vinnie, that was his name." Ally nodded as she explained about Becca and her family arriving at the burnt barn.

"I'm sorry, Ally. There won't be time to rebuild the barn for your wedding next week." Charlotte took a sharp breath. "We'll need to figure out a new place to have it!"

"I'm not worried about any of that." Ally waved her hand as she sighed. "I can't even think about the wedding right now. I need to find out why Vinnie was in that barn, when he shouldn't have been. And why he was dead inside that barn. I need to know who and what started that fire. And why."

"Ally, I think it's great that you want to help, but really sometimes you have to think of yourself, too." Charlotte peered into her eyes. "Don't you want to think about rescheduling all of the plans for the wedding?"

"It can wait. At least until tomorrow. Today, I want to focus on Vinnie. I want to find out what happened." Ally shook her head. "Luke will be investigating, of course, but it doesn't hurt to have a second pair of eyes on the investigation, right?"

"Right." Charlotte nodded. "Then let's see what we can figure out. Where can we start?"

"Why was he there?" Ally tapped her fingertips on the counter. "His future wife, her father, and her cousin, all seemed to be surprised that he was in the barn. Why would he go out to the venue without telling any of them? Also, the owner, Blake, didn't know that he was there. Wouldn't he have called ahead to let Blake know that he wanted to look things over?" She frowned. "Luke and I did get there a little early to walk around, but Vinnie must have been there quite early, because his appointment was after ours, and the barn had been on fire for some time when we arrived. Blake was already there, he must have seen the fire and driven down hoping that he could stop it."

"Did he do anything?" Charlotte started a fresh pot of coffee. "Did you notice anything about him that would indicate he had gone inside the barn or attempted to put the fire out?"

"No, not really." Ally looked up at the ceiling and tried to recall the exact conversation she had with Blake. "His clothes weren't dirty. He seemed very upset. He did say the barn was already on fire when he arrived. He said that was it, he would lose everything." She sighed as she looked back down at the counter. "I guess, this is tragic in more ways than one." Ally knew that Blake and his wife had spent a lot of time and money a couple of years ago turning the old barn into a wedding venue. The setting was beautiful and it had taken a while to get off the ground, but now it was popular and had brought in couples from around the country.

"It is. And no one else was there when you got there?" Charlotte frowned. "That barn is so off the beaten path, I guess it's not likely that anyone would be nearby."

"Not anyone that I saw." Ally took a breath of the coffee-scented air. "It's possible that someone was there, and I didn't notice, because my focus was on the fire. But I didn't hear any other vehicles."

"What do we know about Vinnie?" Charlotte poured them both a mug of coffee and handed one to Ally.

"Nothing, at the moment." Ally frowned. "He was new to the area, I believe. I don't think too many people had gotten to know him."

"And his future wife? Does she live here, too?"

"I don't know." Ally shook her head. "I guess I should have asked a few more questions."

"Alright, that's where our focus needs to be then. In order to find out why Vinnie was at the barn early, we need to figure out what he was up to this morning, and maybe yesterday. We need to know more about him." Charlotte picked up the phone behind the counter. "Luckily, I know just who to ask." She winked. "If Becca was using Morgan as her dress designer, I'm sure that Morgan will have at least some of the details we need. Plus, I'll need to inform her about the wedding." She paused as she met Ally's eyes. "Delayed?"

"For the moment." Ally nodded. "At least until all of this is settled."

Charlotte frowned, then nodded as she turned her attention back to the phone.

Ally sipped her coffee while her grandmother chatted on the phone with Morgan. Her thoughts traveled back to the moment that she'd seen the barn on fire. The shock she'd felt then, had been nothing compared to the shock she felt when Craig had announced that a body had been found. Why hadn't Vinnie left the barn or called for help before the fire engulfed the barn? Maybe he was unconscious so he couldn't. As she recalled the interior of the barn she thought of the large light fittings that hung from the high ceiling. Was it possible that one of them fell and knocked him out?

Ally heard the subtle click of the phone being hung up, and turned toward her grandmother.

"Well?"

"She did design Becca's dress, but she didn't know too much, surprisingly. She did say that Vinnie had been living in Mainbry. She wasn't sure where Becca is living. Vinnie was living in a big house with a good amount of land. She wasn't sure if he owned it or was renting. Becca's family is in from out of town, for the wedding, and they were staying at a hotel. She thinks that now they're all staying in Vinnie's house." Charlotte shook her head. "She did say that it seemed to her that Vinnie went out of his way to avoid conversations, and spending time with other people in the community. Apparently, a few of his neighbors gave him gifts when he first moved in, but he never said much more than a word to them."

"Interesting. Not everyone is as friendly as the people around here are, it's possible that he just preferred to be left alone." Ally narrowed her eyes. "But it's also possible that he had something to hide."

"I would guess the person who would know the most about that would be Becca, but I doubt she's ready to talk about anything right now." Charlotte frowned. "Even if we find out what happened to Vinnie and why he was there, it won't change the tragedy of what has happened."

"You're right, I guess it won't." Ally sighed. "But I still want to find out as much as we can."

"I agree, we need to get this solved. And I think we need to relax in order to do that." Charlotte turned on a radio behind the counter. "As you know, whenever I needed to sort my thoughts out when I ran the shop, I would turn on some music, and just go with the beat to help clear my mind and brighten my mood."

"I'm not sure that will work today." Ally watched as her grandmother danced around the counter toward her.

"Don't know until you try." Charlotte smiled as she grabbed Ally's hand and pulled her to her feet. She pulled Ally close, then spun her away, just as the door to the shop swung open.

Ally gasped as she bumped into Luke mid-spin.

"Luke, how are you?" She smiled, a little dizzy

from the spin, as he let the door fall closed behind him.

"I'm okay." Luke laughed.

"Any news?" Ally asked.

"Preliminary findings from the medical examiner have shown that this wasn't an accident, Vinnie was definitely killed before the fire started. They are going to have to do more testing to be sure, but as it stands now, we're not looking at an accidental death."

"You mean he was murdered?" Ally's eyes widened as she looked over at her grandmother, then back at Luke. "Before the fire even started?"

"Yes, it looks that way. My guess is the fire was started in an attempt to cover up the murder. But I'm not sure of that, yet. It is possible that it could have been a coincidence, but from what Dom has told me, his guess is that as hot as the fire was burning, there was likely some accelerant involved."

"Murder and arson." Charlotte's lips tightened as she shook her head. "Who would do such a thing?"

"That's what I'm looking into now." Luke met Ally's eyes as he took her hand. "Ally, I'm sorry. I know that our wedding plans have been thrown into chaos, but I'm not sure that there's anything I can do to help right now. I have to focus on this investigation."

"Of course you do, Luke." Ally smiled. "You do whatever you have to do, to find the truth. Don't worry one second about the wedding. We'll just delay it until we are ready."

"Aren't you disappointed?" Luke searched her eyes.

"Sure, I guess. But we're still going to have a wedding. It's just going to be a little delayed." Ally shrugged. "The most important thing is to find out the truth for Becca."

"Absolutely." Luke smiled slightly.

"Did the medical examiner have any idea how Vinnie was killed?" Ally glanced over at her grandmother.

"She believes he was strangled, but she's still doing more tests." Luke nodded. "It's possible Vinnie died a few hours before he was found."

"What about his phone?" Charlotte's eyes widened. "Ally and I were just talking about where he might have been, or who he might have spoken to this morning."

"His phone was found, but it had been damaged from the water. We're working on getting what records we can." Luke kissed Ally's cheek. "I need to get back."

"I know you do." Ally hugged him and handed him the keys to his car. "Catch up with you later?"

"For sure." Luke smiled as he looked at her for a lingering moment, then turned and headed back out the door.

Ally watched as the door closed behind him.

"Who was this Vinnie?" She turned to face her grandmother. "Who was he that someone decided to murder him so close to his wedding? Why would anyone do it in that barn?"

"Let's take it one step at a time." Charlotte leaned back against the counter. "It's time we get to know everything we can about Vinnie, and Becca. I'll have Mrs. Bing, Mrs. Cale and Mrs. White come in. I'm sure they will have something to share with us."

"I'll make sure we have plenty of samples in the tray." Ally walked around the counter and began filling the glass sample tray with candies. She frowned as she realized that she would have to break the news to the three women who had been like family to her since she was a little girl. They had been so excited about the wedding, she doubted that they would take the news easily.

CHAPTER 5

*W*ithin minutes the front door swung open, and three women in their seventies marched into the shop, each one with a taller and fancier hat than the last.

Mrs. Bing fluffed the shawl she had draped over her shoulders, then huffed. "I cannot fathom how a murder has taken place in our sweet little town." She plopped down on one of the barstools at the counter. "My, my, my, what have we come to?"

"It's not as if it's never happened before." Mrs. White rolled her eyes as she sat down on the next stool. She set her small purse down on the counter. "It does happen now and then, in every town. And we've had our fair share as well."

"Mrs. Bing is right, we certainly can't allow this

to become a trend around here." Mrs. Cale pulled off her feather-laden hat and set it on the empty stool beside the one she sat down on. "We must stop this kind of behavior before it spreads."

"It's not a disease!" Mrs. White pursed her lips. "We don't even know if the murderer is still in town, do we Charlotte?" She met Charlotte's eyes just as she placed a mug of coffee down in front of her.

"No, we don't. We can't know that. We have no idea who killed Vinnie yet, which is why I called you." Charlotte placed mugs of coffee down in front of Mrs. Bing, and Mrs. Cale.

"I don't know a lot about Vinnie. All I really know is he was new to Mainbry. He was very private. Didn't talk to his neighbors, that sort of thing." Mrs. Bing clucked her tongue. "Now, I wish I had found out much more about him."

"You said he was very private." Ally pushed the sample tray toward the three. "There was probably not much more you could have found out."

"Oh, she has her ways." Mrs. White waved her hand and smiled.

"Nosy, nosy, nosy." Mrs. Cale blew on her coffee.

"You call it nosy, I call it neighborhood watch." Mrs. Bing picked up one of the candies.

"What about Becca? Do any of you know her?"

41

Ally looked between the three women. "Had you noticed her acting strangely in the past few days?"

"I know Becca." Mrs. White nodded. "I spoke to her about hiring a musician for her wedding. I gave her a few recommendations. She didn't seem the least bit concerned about price, but she did say she wanted someone traditional. I'm assuming the ceremony they planned was going to be a bit of a serious occasion."

"Nothing like yours, Ally." Mrs. Cale smiled. "I can't wait for the fun to begin!"

"About that." Ally took a deep breath.

"About what?" Mrs. Bing narrowed her eyes.

"About the wedding." Ally prepared herself for their responses. "We're going to have to postpone."

"What?" Mrs. White's sharp tone drew the attention of everyone else. "Ally, that's ridiculous. There is no reason we can't just find you a new venue."

"No, you don't understand. There won't be any wedding. At least not yet." Ally shook her head. "I can't even think about it. Not until we know what happened to Vinnie."

"No wedding?" Mrs. Bing swayed on her barstool. "No, this can't be happening!"

"Steady there, friend." Mrs. Cale wrapped an arm

around Mrs. Bing to keep her upright. "Ally's right. It wouldn't be fair to her, or anyone else to try to celebrate during a time like this. Her wedding should be a joyful day, with no shadows hanging over it."

"My my!" Mrs. Bing gasped as she stared at Ally. "Well then, we must find the culprit quickly, mustn't we?"

"Where do we start?" Mrs. Cale picked up one of the salted caramel candies. "Shall we interrogate the suspects?"

"We don't have any suspects, yet." Mrs. White rolled her eyes.

"Oh, I disagree." Mrs. Bing snapped her fingers. "There's the fiancée. In cases like this, it's always the fiancée, isn't it?"

"Becca?" Ally narrowed her eyes. "She was distraught. She lost someone she loved. I'm not so sure she should be a suspect."

"Or was it an act?" Mrs. Cale leaned forward as she whispered, "I saw this once on one of my favorite soap operas. The woman murdered her husband, but not before she took acting classes to make sure that she could play the role of a grieving widow!"

"Wow." Charlotte raised an eyebrow. "That's dedication."

"It's also fiction." Mrs. White crossed her arms. "Can we take this seriously please?"

"She's not wrong." Mrs. Cale shrugged. "We don't know too much about Vinnie, yet, but we do know that he wasn't the most pleasant man to be around. Maybe their relationship wasn't about love. Maybe he was cheating on her, and she found out."

"In that case you might consider the father and cousin, too." Charlotte mused. "They may have wanted to get revenge if their loved one was hurt."

"She didn't seem hurt." Ally shook her head as she recalled the scene at the barn. "She seemed devastated by his death."

"Acting!" Mrs. Cale stuck her pinky finger up into the air as she took a sip of her coffee. "We need to find out more about their relationship."

"Yes, we do." Charlotte nodded. "I think I know a way we can at least get a chance to talk with her. We can make her a sympathy basket. With candies, and flowers."

"We can use some of the flowers from my order at the florist. I'm sure it's too late to cancel or get a refund, at least for most of them, so they might as well go to a good cause." Ally shrugged.

"But what if we solve this today, and you can get married tomorrow?" Mrs. Bing frowned. "You'll need those flowers."

"That's a nice thought, Mrs. Bing, but I really don't think we'll solve this today. Besides, I can always order more flowers." Ally glanced up at the clock. "It's about time to close up the shop. I'll head over to the florist and pick up the flowers, then we can put the basket together. Thanks, Mee-Maw, this is a great idea."

"Hopefully, it will get us inside." Mrs. Cale smirked. "Then we can interrogate the suspect."

"Oh, I think it might be better if just Ally and I deliver the basket." Charlotte smiled. "It might seem a bit overwhelming if we all go."

"Fine." Mrs. Cale sighed. "But before all of this is over, I am going to interrogate someone! There's a new character on my favorite soap, and she's a great detective."

"This is real life, remember?" Mrs. White nudged her shoulder.

"Oh, I need a new hat! A detective can't wear such a fancy hat." Mrs. Cale frowned as she looked over her hat. "It's too distracting."

"Yes, that is the first sign of a great detective, deciding which hat to wear." Mrs. White laughed.

CINDY BELL

"Ignore her, darling." Mrs. Bing took Mrs. Cale's arm. "We'll just do a quick shop for something more detective-esque."

Ally stepped out of the shop as the three continued to bicker with each other. Although the three had been best friends for as long as she could remember, they acted more like siblings, with their teasing. However, she'd seen their true bond shine through more than once, whenever one of them was in trouble.

As Ally walked down the street toward the florist, her mind shifted to their theory. Could Becca have been involved in Vinnie's murder? It didn't seem likely, since she had arrived with her father and cousin. But if Vinnie had been killed before the fire, she would have had time to kill him, and then meet up with her father and cousin.

Ally stepped into the florist and found Tanya at the front counter, deep in conversation with Gloria.

"You know there can't be a wedding, now, how can you not give us a refund on the flowers?"

"It's just not that simple, I'm sorry." Gloria's voice reached a high-pitched level that Ally had never heard from her before. "I already purchased the flowers, I can't return them, and they can't be used for any other event while they are still fresh. I would have to pay for them out of my own pocket. I can't be expected to take that big of a loss, can I?"

"Have you no compassion?" Tanya's voice hardened. "My cousin has lost her fiancé today, and she asked me to carry out these tasks for her so that she wouldn't have to think about it. Now, I have to go back to her and tell her that she has to pay for flowers for a wedding that will never happen?"

"I'm sure you can work something out." Ally stepped forward.

The two looked over at her with surprise, as if they hadn't noticed her entrance.

"Excuse me?" Gloria met her eyes.

"Maybe you could use the flowers for the funeral," Ally suggested.

"Maybe." Tanya nodded at Ally. "I know that you have your own troubles to worry about. I've heard that you're not having your wedding."

"You have?" Ally looked from Tanya, to Gloria.

"It's getting around town." Gloria nodded. "It started as a rumor."

"This town." Ally rolled her eyes. "There are no secrets here."

Gloria sighed. "I'm sorry, I know it sounds heartless of me not to refund the flowers, but the shop hasn't been open for long, and it hasn't been very successful yet."

"It's fine." Tanya held up her hands. "It's not your fault that the wedding was canceled. Let me see if I can talk Becca into using them for the funeral. That is a good idea."

"I could change the arrangements to make them more appropriate, if you'd like. No charge." Gloria met her eyes. "I truly am sorry."

"Thank you, that would be helpful." Tanya nodded to Ally, then walked out of the shop.

Ally turned her attention to Gloria. "If you wouldn't mind, I'd like to take a few of the flowers from my order. Just one bunch. You already have some, right?"

"Yes, I do. The rest are coming in the next couple of days. Do you want me to cancel what I can?"

"Yes please." Ally nodded.

"I'll see what I can do." Gloria walked over to a glass enclosure and stepped inside. She returned with a bunch of flowers. "Will this be enough?"

"Yes, thank you." Ally took the flowers. "Gloria, I'm sorry all of this has happened, I'm sure it won't be easy on your business with all of the weddings that had been planned at the barn canceled."

"No, it won't be." Gloria took a deep breath. "But

that's not what matters really, is it?" She shook her head. "Hopefully, one day soon we'll be celebrating your wedding, Ally, and the town can move on from this."

"I hope so."

CHAPTER 6

*lly returned to the shop to find her grandmother hard at work filling a basket with various boxes of candy and other treats.

"Here are the flowers." Ally set the flowers down on the table next to the basket. Her eyes lingered on the colorful blooms.

"They're gorgeous." Charlotte looked up at her.

"They are." Ally picked up the broom that rested against the wall. "I'll sweep up a bit and get the shop ready to close. Why don't you pick out one of Luke's carvings to include in the basket?" Her eyes swept over the assortment of carvings and toys that Luke had created to sell in the shop. Each one had its own unique design.

"That's a lovely idea, Ally." Charlotte nodded.

"Are you meeting Jeff tonight?" Ally smiled. Jeff was also a resident at Freely Lakes. Charlotte had become close to him in the last few years. Ally loved how happy he made her grandmother.

"No, I don't think so. He's been busy filling costume jewelry orders." Charlotte glanced at Ally.

"He is so talented."

As Ally swept the front of the shop, she thought about speaking to Becca again. She could be a suspect, but she had to tread carefully. She didn't want to upset her any more than she already was. She tossed the dirt she collected in the dustpan into the trash, then placed the broom back against the wall.

"All set." Charlotte attached a card to the basket, then picked it up. "Oh, it might be a bit too full."

"Let me get that." Ally took the basket from her grandmother. "Yes, you did fill it up, didn't you?" She held the basket with both hands.

"I figured a little bit of everything might be best." Charlotte smiled.

"It's great."

"I'll drive us." Charlotte held open the door for Ally.

"Can you lock up please?"

"Sure." Charlotte locked up and started to walk

toward the car. As she did Cinnamon pranced over to them. The white cat with light brown patches had been taken in by an elderly gentleman, Carlisle, who lived down the street from the shop. Charlotte bent down to stroke Cinnamon's head as he rubbed against Ally's calves before he walked toward his home. "I'm surprised you didn't bring Peaches and Arnold in today."

"I did check on them on the way to the dress shop this morning. Luke and I had so many errands to run, I didn't want Peaches roaming the neighborhood and hitting everyone up for treats." Ally rolled her eyes. "She has the whole block thinking that I'm starving her."

"Oh, no one thinks that." Charlotte laughed as she opened the back door to the car. "They just love seeing her."

Ally set the basket in the backseat, then pulled open the passenger door. "Most do, but sometimes she can wear out her welcome. She was shooed out of the dress shop the other day after mangling some lace. I paid for it of course, but she's been getting into things lately."

"She's probably just excited about the wedding." Charlotte smiled. "Cats know these things."

"Yes, I know she does." Ally thought of all the

discussions she'd had with her cat, who in many ways was more of a best friend than a pet. "Between her and Arnold, I don't get much privacy around the cottage."

"I bet." Charlotte laughed. "I remember those days. That pot-bellied pig would always find a way to get up into bed with me!"

"Maybe because you bought him some steps?" Ally grinned.

"Okay, yes, but only because he's afraid of the dark." Charlotte started the car. "I was able to get the address for Vinnie's house from Mrs. Bing. It's on the outskirts of Mainbry. It's not too far from here."

"Good." Ally looked out through the windshield as her grandmother pulled the car onto the road that led to the neighboring town of Mainbry. "I just keep thinking about Vinnie. What drew him out to that barn? Why did he show up early? How did he end up getting killed there?"

"We actually don't know if he was killed there." Charlotte glanced over at her. "We just know that his body was there. It could have been placed there."

"Then the barn was set on fire. Was it really just to cover things up, or was it some kind of message to Blake?" Ally frowned. "He did say it would ruin him."

"We might be overlooking another unpleasant

possibility." Charlotte pulled the car into a driveway in front of a large house. "Blake could have been the one to set the fire to cover up the murder. You said that you and Luke arrived a little early, maybe he had hoped that the body would be completely destroyed by then."

"Maybe." Ally shivered. "What a terrible thought."

"It is, but one we'll have to consider."

"I still don't think that he could destroy his own barn." Ally shook her head. "He seemed so upset when it was destroyed."

"Maybe he was acting." Charlotte opened the car door.

Ally got out of the car and opened the door to the backseat. "Are you sure about this, Mee-Maw? You don't think they will find it a little strange for us to just show up like this?"

"They might, and they might not let us in at all. But it's worth a try, right?" Charlotte shrugged. "And even if they refuse us, we'll have offered them some comfort, which is better than nothing."

"You're right." Ally picked up the basket and carried it toward the door, with Charlotte a few steps behind her.

Charlotte knocked on the door.

A moment later it swung open. Gus stood in the

doorway. "What's this?" He studied the basket in Ally's hands.

"I was there today, at the fire," Ally stammered as his dark eyes met hers. "I'm so sorry for your loss. I just thought this might bring you and your family some comfort."

"Flowers, and candies?" Gus nodded as he took the basket from her. "Thank you. I'm sure it won't go to waste."

"Papa, who's at the door?" Becca appeared in the doorway. "You!" She glared at Ally. "What are you doing here?"

"Becca, don't be rude." Gus' stern voice quieted the young woman. "These people are just trying to be kind." He sighed as he looked back at them. "I'm very sorry, it's been a hard day for all of us."

"I'm sure it has." Charlotte looked into his eyes. "You lost a wonderful man, and there are so many questions about it. I can only imagine how painful and frustrating that is."

"It is." Becca's suddenly quiet voice drew all of their attention. "I just keep asking myself, how could this happen? Who would kill my Vinnie?"

"We're going to figure that out, Becca." A man stepped up behind her and placed his hand on her shoulder. "Maybe a little company would help right now." He looked at Gus. "Shall we invite them in?"

"I don't know if that's such a good idea, Cliff." Gus shook his head. "I'm not sure that Becca is up for it."

"It's okay." Becca dabbed her eyes with a tissue Cliff offered her. "He's right, maybe it will help to talk a little." She turned and walked toward the living room.

"Alright then, just a short visit." Gus stepped away from the door.

Ally followed Becca toward the living room. She noticed that Cliff kept his hand on Becca's shoulder until she was seated on the couch, then he sat down beside her.

Becca picked up a framed photograph and stared at it.

"Is that Vinnie?" Ally sat down on an easy chair.

Charlotte lingered near Gus, who hovered at the entrance of the living room.

"Yes." Becca turned the photograph around to reveal the image. A man, shorter than most, and thin, beamed at the camera. His handsome features and thick, chestnut hair held Ally's attention. "He was so handsome." Becca gulped, then shook her head. "I still can't get used to talking about him that way."

"I know this must be very difficult." Ally glanced over at her grandmother who had moved toward the kitchen with Gus. She noticed they were discussing something, but she couldn't make out their words.

"I do have to get used to it, though. As Cliff tells me, it's best to face this head on." Becca sniffled. "I'm not even sure that I want to find out what really happened to Vinnie. What difference would it even make? He'll still be gone."

"But won't it give you some comfort to know that the person who did this to him, to both of you, will be behind bars?" Ally looked into her eyes.

"I don't know." Becca's shoulders drooped. "Maybe it will just make it harder, knowing what happened. I wish it was just an accident."

"I can understand that." Ally nodded, then shifted forward to the edge of the couch. "But honestly, Becca, it may be up to you to help figure out what happened."

"Up to her?" Cliff's tone sharpened. "What do you mean by that?"

"I just mean, Becca knew him best. She knew who he spent time with, what he might have been up to, she probably has the most important information for the investigation." Ally met her eyes. "It may be impossible for the police to solve this case, without a little help, since no one else around here knew him very well. I've heard, he was a bit of a loner."

"He just liked his privacy." Becca crossed her arms as she stared at Ally. "You were supposed to marry that cop that was with you today, right? This weekend? At the same place?"

"Yes, I was." Ally frowned. "But we've decided to postpone things."

"Oh?" Becca's eyes widened. "You should take a lesson from my experience, and do it while you still have the chance. Before it's taken away from you."

"I'm sorry you're going through so much, Becca. I just want to help." Ally stood up as she sensed the animosity brewing in Becca's expression. "Maybe it would be better if we leave."

"Yes, I think that would be best." Cliff followed Ally toward the door, where Charlotte joined her. "I'm sorry, I guess she wasn't ready for guests just yet."

"It's fine." Ally smiled slightly. "It's a good thing she has a friend like you."

"We're more like family, we've known each other for so long." Cliff glanced back at Becca, then looked back at the two of them. "It breaks my heart to see her like this. Trying to find Vinnie's killer may be a hopeless effort." His voice was soft.

Ally stared at him as his words sank in.

"It certainly is worth trying, though." Ally studied him a moment longer. "How did you and Becca first meet?"

"We've known each other since we were kids. We dated for a few years. But that's really a story for another time." Cliff opened the door. "Thank you very much for the basket. I think it would be best if you respected the family's wish for privacy."

When the door closed behind them, Charlotte met Ally's eyes. "That seemed a bit rough, what exactly happened in the living room?"

"I learned that they aren't too concerned if the murder is solved." Ally sighed as she walked over to the car. "I know that everyone grieves differently, but I find it odd that Becca doesn't seem more concerned with finding out the truth about what happened to Vinnie."

"She's probably still in shock." Charlotte settled in the driver's seat. "I spoke to Gus a bit. He said that Vinnie was supposed to ride with them to the venue. When they arrived at the house to pick him and Becca up, he wasn't there. Becca insisted that they still go, but she hadn't been able to reach Vinnie to find out where he was."

"Did he say when Becca last saw Vinnie?" Ally

held her breath as her grandmother pulled the car out into the street.

"He said she said she saw him last night, but when she woke up this morning he was already gone. He hadn't left a note. She assumed he had gone out for a run, as he did that sometimes." Charlotte started to turn down the road that would lead them back to the cottage.

"Wait, Mee-Maw. I'm not ready to go back yet. I want to speak to Blake again."

"Okay." Charlotte turned in the opposite direction. "Why is that?"

"I think that there has to be some kind of reason why Vinnie was killed in Blake's barn. Especially if Vinnie didn't tell anyone where he was going. Why would he just disappear and end up in Blake's barn? It doesn't make sense to me. I just want to ask Blake a few questions about it." Ally gazed out through the side window. "It just feels off."

"It does." Charlotte drove past the long driveway that led to the barn. She turned down the next driveway, which led to Blake's farmhouse. "I just hope he's willing to talk about it. Gus mentioned something to me that I thought was a bit strange. He asked the police when the first call about the fire came in. I guess he wanted to get an idea of what happened out there so he could find out what happened to Vinnie. According to what the police told him, you were the only one that called the fire in."

"What?" Ally looked over at her. "Are you saying that Blake never called it in?"

"That appears to be the case." Charlotte parked near the farmhouse. "Apparently, your call was the only one on record."

"I just assumed that he had called because he was there before us and the firetrucks arrived so quickly." Ally narrowed her eyes. "It never crossed my mind that he didn't call."

CHAPTER 7

As Ally and Charlotte stepped out of the car, the front door of Blake's house opened, and Blake stepped out onto the porch.

"Ally? Charlotte? What are you doing here?" He descended the front steps and met them in the driveway.

"Just wanted to check on you." Ally smiled at him. "I know it's been a very rough day, and I left earlier without really getting a chance to make sure you were okay. You've been so kind to Luke and me while we planned our wedding."

"Ally, I'm so sorry that all of this happened." Blake pulled off his cowboy hat and wrapped his hands around the brim. "I know that you were counting on the barn for the wedding. I wish we could work something else out for you, but everything is so crazy at the moment."

"I understand, I'm not concerned about the wedding. I really want to help figure out what happened to Vinnie." Ally met his eyes. "Would you be willing to talk to me about what you saw today?"

"What can I say about it?" Blake sighed. "You saw the same thing I did. The barn was on fire."

"You say you saw the barn on fire, but from what I understand when we arrived, you hadn't called the fire department yet, why was that?" Ally held his gaze.

"What?" Blake blinked, then shook his head. "I was in shock, I guess. I saw the smoke, then the flames, and I didn't know what to do."

"Did you try to put it out?" Ally kept her tone even as he shifted from one foot to the other.

"How could I? It was such a huge fire. There was no way that I could put it out." Blake cleared his throat.

"It's probably for the best that you didn't put yourself at risk. Did you manage to see inside? Maybe notice anything knocked over or strange around the outside of the barn?" Ally tried to meet his eyes, in the same moment that he took a step back.

"What is this?" Blake stared at her. "Why are you asking me all of these questions?"

"You're the closest there is to an eyewitness of the murder, Blake." Charlotte spoke in a casual tone. "What you may have seen or heard before the police arrived could be exactly what cracks the case."

"I didn't see or hear anything unusual." Blake frowned. "I just saw the fire, and that was all I could think about, all my life's work going up in flames." He wiped at his eyes. "You aren't the only one planning to cancel your wedding. Everyone I had lined up for the next two months has called to cancel. That's the entire wedding season!"

"I understand you were upset." Ally looked into his eyes. "It had to be frightening to see the barn on fire like that, after you had taken precautions to prevent that from happening. Did you have any other visitors this morning? Anyone that might have pulled in, then turned around and left?"

"I have no idea." Blake shook his head. "I didn't have any earlier appointments, so I hadn't even been down to the barn this morning." He frowned. "But I did notice a flash of headlights on the road late last night. We don't get too many people out here that late. I was just getting ready for bed and I noticed the headlights through the living room window."

"What time was that?" Charlotte stepped forward.

"I'd guess it was a little after midnight, but I don't know exactly." Blake sighed. "It could have just been one of the neighbors' kids coming home from a party or something. I didn't think much about it."

"Thanks Blake." Ally glanced at the sky as it began to darken. "It's been a long day. I hope you're able to get some rest."

"Me too." Blake placed his hat back on his head, then watched as they returned to their car.

Ally frowned as Charlotte turned the car around in the driveway.

"Something still seems off to me. I think if I saw anything of mine on fire, my first instinct would be to call for help. Wouldn't it be yours?"

"I think so, but I've never been in that situation, so I can't say for sure." Charlotte turned back onto the main road. "People do react to shock in different ways, but I agree with you, it's odd."

"At least we know that someone else was in the area just after midnight. That might be something that Luke can look into. There aren't many traffic cameras around, but maybe someone else along the road saw something."

"That's definitely possible." Charlotte patted her knee.

"I just want the pieces to fit." Ally stared hard through the windshield. "So far we know that Becca isn't telling us everything. It seems as if she has a reason to refuse to cooperate with the police. Blake behaved oddly when he saw his barn on fire. That's not a lot to go on."

"It's just a start. Maybe Luke will have come up with something by the morning." Charlotte glanced over at her. "I'm going to see if Jeff is available for dinner tonight. Do you want to join us?"

"No, thanks Mee-Maw." Ally smiled. "I just want to snuggle up with Arnold and Peaches and get some sleep."

"Okay, why don't I drop you off at the cottage and I'll pick you up in the morning? We can open the shop together?" Charlotte nodded.

"Are you sure? I can manage the shop alone, you can have the day off."

"Not a chance, we have chocolates to make and a murder to solve." Charlotte laughed.

When they reached the small cottage she had grown up in with her grandmother, and now lived in as an adult, Ally's body ached for the comfort of her bed, and the familiar sounds of her pets. As soon as she opened the door, she heard Peaches' claws against the wooden floor, and Arnold's squeals from the kitchen.

"Oh, I've missed you, too!" Ally scooped the orange cat up into her arms and nuzzled her cheek with her own.

Arnold skidded across the wood floor as he bolted in their direction.

"Hi buddy." Charlotte patted his head, then stroked Peaches' back. "I just wanted to say hello, but I have to get going." She gave Peaches, Arnold and Ally a kiss goodbye.

"Have a good night, Mee-Maw." Ally waved to her as she headed down the driveway.

"I plan to." Charlotte glanced over her shoulder.

When her grandmother was in the car, Ally closed the cottage door. With Peaches still in her arms she turned toward Arnold.

"I bet you two are starving. I'm sorry, I didn't mean to be away for so long." Ally patted Arnold's head as he snorted at her. "Let's go get you both some dinner."

Once they had been fed, Ally grabbed some leftovers from the fridge and plopped down on the couch.

Peaches jumped up on the back of it and walked over to rub against the side of Ally's head.

Ally relaxed at the sound of her purr. "Oh Peaches, it's been a long day."

Peaches curled up along her shoulders and purred even louder.

Despite the events of the day, all of the tension in Ally's body began to melt away.

～

First thing in the morning, Ally heard a light knock at her door.

She opened one eye, then the other.

She heard the lock click on her front door.

Her heartbeat quickened.

"Ally?" Her grandmother's voice wafted through the cottage. "Are you up?"

Peaches bolted off of the bed to greet Charlotte. Arnold followed at a slower pace behind her.

Ally pushed herself up and wiped at her eyes. "Be out in a minute, Mee-Maw." She yawned as she glanced at the clock. She'd had a hard time getting to sleep the night before, and had slept an hour later than usual.

"I'm so sorry, did I wake you?" Charlotte called

out from the kitchen. "I knew I should have called first!"

Ally smiled at the sounds of her grandmother preparing the coffee maker.

"It's okay, Mee-Maw, I'm glad you came. I'll be right out." Ally dressed, then joined her grandmother just as the coffee maker began to drip. "I didn't mean to sleep so late, I just had a hard time falling asleep last night."

"I can't imagine why." Charlotte frowned as she cupped her cheeks and looked into her eyes. "Are you sure you don't want to go back to sleep? I can open the shop."

"Absolutely not. Let's take Arnold and Peaches in today." Ally smiled. "What do you think?"

"Yes, they must be due for an outing." Charlotte dropped her hands to her sides.

"Last night, while I was thinking about the case, I realized that there's one person we should really speak to." Ally popped two halves of a bagel into the toaster. "Blake's wife, Marie. He claims he was at home with her when the fire broke out, but we haven't heard that from her, have we?"

"Good point." Charlotte grabbed two plates, along with the butter dish, and set them on the table. "Do you think she'll say something different?"

CINDY BELL

"I'm not sure. I hate to think that Blake could be involved in this, but it still seems odd that the murder, or at least the attempted cover-up of the murder would take place in his barn, if there wasn't something to it." Ally grabbed the bagel out of the toaster and set one half on each plate.

Arnold trotted into the kitchen with his nose in the air.

"Oh, there's food, huh?" Charlotte grinned as she crouched down to pet him. "I miss you so much, my little Arnold. I do wish I could have taken you with me when I moved into Freely Lakes."

"Well, there was that time you tried to smuggle him in." Ally grinned as she grabbed a few treats for Arnold to munch on. "It didn't go too well, remember?"

"Yes, he's a bit too big and snorts a bit too much to pass off as my grandbaby." Charlotte laughed as she spread some butter across her bagel. "Okay, so we're going to try to talk with Marie?"

"Yes, this afternoon?" Ally took the knife from her grandmother and buttered her bagel.

"Great, after we close up."

After they had finished breakfast, Ally attached Arnold and Peaches' leashes to their harnesses and the four of them walked toward the car.

Arnold squealed with excitement when he jumped into the car. He lay on the backseat and Peaches curled up on Ally's lap. Ally stroked her head as Peaches drifted off to sleep.

"They do love an outing." Charlotte smiled as she pulled onto the road that led to the shop.

"They do." Ally laughed as Arnold snored loudly.

"Once they've had a nap first, though." Charlotte turned into the parking lot of Charlotte's Chocolate Heaven.

"It looks like we have company." Ally smiled at the sight of the three women clustered around the door of the shop.

"Ally! Charlotte! There you are!" Mrs. White waved to them as they walked up to the door with Arnold and Peaches on their leashes.

"Hi piggy." Mrs. Bing grinned as she patted Arnold's head.

"We just have to put them in the courtyard, then we'll open up." Ally gestured around the back.

Ally and Charlotte guided Arnold and Peaches to the fenced-in courtyard that had a pigpen set up for Arnold. As soon as they were let off their leashes, Peaches started chasing Arnold around in circles.

"That's obviously their favorite game at the

moment." Ally laughed as she followed her grandmother back around to the front door.

"Oh, we turned up something good!" Mrs. Cale looked at them as she rubbed her hands together.

"Calm down, you might start a fire with those dried-out hands!" Mrs. White huffed.

Charlotte slid the key into the lock and opened the door to the shop.

"Dry hands?" Mrs. Cale gasped. "I'll have you know I follow a very strict skin care regimen!"

"Someone has been looking for Vinnie!" The words burst from Mrs. Bing's mouth as the two other women continued to squabble.

CHAPTER 8

"What?" Ally looked between Mrs. Bing, Mrs. Cale and Mrs. White. "What do you mean someone has been looking for Vinnie?"

"Not just someone." Mrs. White narrowed her eyes. "A very suspicious character. A fellow that people around town have been trying to avoid, because he gives off a rather dishonest aura."

"That's putting it nicely." Mrs. Cale smiled. "We asked around town in Mainbry and Mrs. Donovan at the laundromat said that he looked seedier than a bag of birdseed!"

"She said that?" Ally's eyes widened as she tried to hold back a laugh.

"Well, maybe not that exactly, but it was something like that." Mrs. Cale nodded as she sat down on a barstool at the counter. "She was quite frightened of him, almost called the police, just because of the way he looked at her."

"That seems a little extreme." Charlotte turned on the coffee maker. "Is it possible that he's just new in town?"

"Trust me, there's a difference between newcomers, and bad apples." Mrs. White pursed her lips. "From what I've heard, he's as slick as his hairstyle, and there's a good chance that he had something to do with Vinnie's murder." She crossed her arms. "Now, we just have to find him, then we can be on with the wedding."

"Wait just a moment." Ally held up one finger. "First of all, you can't judge a person's intentions simply by the way they look, that's absolutely unacceptable. Secondly, just because you suspect this person, that certainly doesn't make him the killer."

"You listen to me, young lady." Mrs. Cale tapped her own forehead. "I know something is up, and I'm never wrong. We need to get our hands on this guy fast, before someone else ends up dead."

"Have you told Luke about this?" Ally picked up her phone.

"Not yet, we thought we'd run it by you first." Mrs. White scrunched up her nose. "He can be a little cranky sometimes, when he's working a case."

"True." Charlotte nodded as she put a sample tray of chocolates in front of the ladies.

"Mee-Maw!" Ally shot a look in her direction, then finished sending a text to Luke. "Alright, I've let him know to be on the lookout for this man. I don't suppose anyone got his name?"

"He never gives it." Mrs. Bing narrowed her eyes as she popped a nut cluster into her mouth. "That's the strangest part, isn't it? He just asks about Vinnie, then walks away. No name, no contact number, nothing."

"Interesting." Ally glanced over at Charlotte. "Maybe it's time we run into this stranger."

"If he's even still in town." Charlotte crossed her arms. "If he did have something to do with the murder, I doubt that he'd be hanging around, waiting to get caught."

"Oh, good point." Mrs. Bing nodded, then helped herself to another nut cluster. "But if he is still around, maybe we can get him to confess."

"How are we going to do that?" Mrs. White raised an eyebrow.

"We'll just have to set a trap for him." Mrs. Bing smiled. "Simple as that."

"That doesn't sound all that simple." Mrs. Cale shook her head as she popped a milk chocolate covered hazelnut into her mouth.

"Let's take it one step at a time, ladies." Charlotte grabbed an order pad and pen from beside the register. "Who was the first person who saw this stranger?"

"I'd say it was probably Bobby at the grocery store. He said he saw him on Tuesday morning. He bought a newspaper, and a small bottle of milk. Bobby thought it was odd because most people would stop by a smaller shop for that. The man asked him about Vinnie. Bobby said Vinnie is in there once a week to buy a few groceries, usually the same stuff. But he didn't feel right about telling the stranger anything about Vinnie, so he lied and said he didn't know him." Mrs. Cale frowned. "Even Bobby noticed that he had that untrustworthy nature, but that's not surprising, since Bobby notices just about everything."

"Did he use a credit card to pay?" Ally raised her eyebrows.

"No, he paid with cash." Mrs. Cale shook her head. "I did think to ask that."

"Too bad." Ally frowned as she placed mugs of coffee in front of the three ladies. "Who spotted him next?"

"Mrs. Donovan, at the laundromat, saw him later that day. He came in and asked her about Vinnie, but didn't wash any clothes." Mrs. White added some cream to her coffee. "Mrs. Donovan didn't know Vinnie from the laundromat, but she had seen him and Becca at the coffee shop in town a few times. She did tell the stranger about that, and then he left."

"Do we know what time he went to the laundromat?" Charlotte made a note on her order pad.

"It was in the afternoon." Mrs. Bing took a sip of her coffee. "Just after the lunch hour rush at the laundromat."

"Anyone else?" Ally peered at the notes Charlotte made.

"We stopped in at the coffee shop and asked the staff about anyone who came in looking for Vinnie. One of the waitresses, Linda, said that the stranger had been there, ordered only a cup of coffee, and asked her about Vinnie." Mrs. Cale sighed. "She was hoping for a good tip, so she told him where Vinnie lived."

"Oh dear." Charlotte gasped.

"So, whoever this stranger is, knew where Vinnie lived." Ally narrowed her eyes. "That makes him quite a good suspect. But if he knew where he lived, why would he kill him at the barn?"

"He might have moved the body to direct suspicion away from himself." Mrs. Cale popped a piece of fudge in her mouth.

"He's only a good suspect, if we can manage to figure out who he is." Charlotte shook her head. "Did he happen to tell the waitress where he might be staying?"

"No, she said he didn't even leave her a tip, just paid for the coffee and left, without even drinking it." Mrs. White picked up one of the white chocolate caramel candies. "She said he left in a rush."

"How did they describe him?" Ally asked.

"Tall and wide." Mrs. Cale held her hands above her head, then out to the side. "Very muscular."

"Slicked-back hair." Mrs. White ran her hand back over the top of her head.

"And a mustache." Mrs. Bing nodded.

"Luke's going to want to know all about this." Ally picked up her phone just as the front door to the shop opened.

"No need to call, it seems." Charlotte smiled as Luke stepped through the door.

"Oh, we'll just be off!" Mrs. Bing grabbed Mrs. Cale's hand and tugged her toward the side door.

Mrs. White followed right behind them.

"I thought I'd stop in and give you an update." Luke eyed the coffee pot. "Do you have any of that peppermint coffee brewed?"

"Of course, I always keep one going just for you." Ally smiled as she poured some coffee into a mug.

Luke glanced back at the door. "What was with those three? They ran out of here like I might chase after them."

"They're a little nervous about how focused you get during an investigation." Ally set the mug down in front of him. "But they're the ones who gave me the information about the stranger in town. Did you manage to come up with something about him?"

"I haven't had much time to look into it. With no name, and not much of a description, no." Luke shook his head, then blew across the surface of his coffee. "But I am doing my best to look into Vinnie's phone records. His phone was destroyed by the water from extinguishing the fire, but I should still be able to find out who he was recently in touch with. It would be a lot easier if Becca was willing to help me, but she refuses to give me any of Vinnie's personal information."

"That's strange, isn't it? Shouldn't she want to find his killer?" Ally slid a box of his favorite candies over to him. "I'm sure you're starving."

"Even if I'm not, these are impossible to resist." Luke pulled the lid off and grabbed a milk chocolate from inside. "Thank you, Ally."

"Sweets for my sweet." Ally winked at him, then leaned on the counter. "So, why don't you think Becca wants to help?"

"Oh right, sorry. Distracted." Luke ate another milk chocolate, then looked into her eyes. "Whatever the reason that Becca doesn't want to help, I still managed to dig up some information about Vinnie's past. It's been very hard to find anything going back further than two years, but I didn't have to look too far to discover another tragedy in his life. Less than a year ago, a man he listed as his business partner, disappeared. It is suspected he was murdered. Not far from here, actually. The crime hasn't been solved. I spoke to the detective handling the case, and he said he had absolutely nowhere to go with it. No surprise, he also said that Vinnie was not very cooperative with him."

"Wow, Luke, do you think whoever killed his partner, might have killed Vinnie, too?" Ally's eyes widened. "Maybe he was looking for Vinnie this whole time. Maybe he's the stranger."

"It's possible. His business partner just disappeared and is presumed murdered." Luke tipped his head to the side. "It's a strange coincidence for them both to be killed in less than a year. My guess is whatever business they were involved in, wasn't the business they listed on their paperwork. I get the feeling Vinnie was involved in some criminal activity."

"What makes you think that?" Ally frowned. "Just because his partner was probably murdered? The withholding of information?"

"I can find records of his wealth, but not exactly where that wealth came from. That usually means that the money is coming from an illegal source. Of course, I don't have enough to prove that yet, but it's making me rethink who might have been involved in his murder." Luke met her eyes. "It could explain why Becca doesn't want to talk, too. If she knew about his illegal activities, then maybe she's afraid she could get in trouble for them."

"Or that she could be a target, too." Ally's eyes widened at the thought. "What if Vinnie's killer isn't done yet?"

"Without Becca telling me the truth, I'm not sure that there's much I can do to protect her. But I will keep an eye on her." Luke glanced toward the door. "I should get going."

"Wait." Charlotte pulled the piece of paper off of the order pad and handed it to Luke. "Here is a list of where the stranger was seen. Maybe you can build some kind of timeline with it, and figure out who else he might have spoken to."

"Great idea, Charlotte." Luke took the list from her. "Thank you both. I appreciate your help with all of this." He paused at the door and looked back at them. "Please, be careful, though. Ally is right, it's possible that whoever wanted to get rid of Vinnie still has some plans here in town."

"We will be." Ally sighed as the door closed behind him. "Mee-Maw, this is getting more complicated by the minute."

"I agree." Charlotte frowned. "I wonder exactly what Vinnie was involved in."

"Maybe we should try to talk to Becca again, or her cousin Tanya. I bet one of them has to know what Vinnie was up to."

"We will, but let's see if we can speak to Marie first."

"Yes, I'll call her right now. I spoke to her a few

times while we planned the wedding. She seemed very sweet." Ally picked up her phone and dialed the number she had stored for Marie. "I'll try to arrange to meet her this afternoon."

"Good morning, this is Marie." She answered the phone.

"Hi Marie, this is Ally."

"Oh Ally, I'm so sorry. You must be so disappointed about the wedding."

"It's alright, really. Do you think my grandmother and I could come over this afternoon, around two thirty? Would you have a few minutes to talk? I just want to iron a few things out." Ally stopped short of mentioning the wedding.

"Of course, anything I can do to help. I'll be here."

"Great, thanks so much." Ally ended the call, then nodded to Charlotte. "She sounded okay with speaking to us."

"Hopefully, she will be more willing to share information than Becca was." Charlotte narrowed her eyes.

"I've been thinking about the illegal business that Vinnie might have been caught up in. I thought maybe if Becca knew about it, she might be a bit frightened. But she didn't strike me as frightened."

"No, she didn't seem afraid to me, either. But maybe she's hiding it." Charlotte shrugged.

"Maybe Luke will get something out of her."

"Hopefully." Charlotte nodded.

CHAPTER 9

*C*harlotte's Chocolate Heaven was quiet for the rest of the morning. After locking up and dropping Peaches and Arnold at home, Charlotte and Ally headed out to talk to Marie at the farmhouse.

"Blake's truck isn't here." Ally tipped her head toward the empty parking spot. "Just Marie's car."

"That's a relief, maybe she'll share more with us if he isn't around." Charlotte glanced over at Ally.

"If there is anything to share." Ally stepped out of her car and waited for her grandmother to join her.

As they neared the porch, Marie opened the front door.

"Come in, ladies, I've made us some coffee." She left the door open for them.

Ally stepped inside the familiar living room. Blake and Marie had invited her there to discuss the wedding more than once. She loved the fact that they treated her wedding more like a family affair than a business transaction.

"Here we go." Marie set a tray down on the coffee table, with three mugs and containers of cream and sugar. As she straightened up, she looked into Ally's eyes. "How are you doing? Really?"

"I'm okay, thanks Marie." Ally smiled as she sat down on the couch.

Charlotte sat down beside her.

"Thank you so much for the coffee." Charlotte picked up her mug. "We're just wondering how you're holding up."

"Oh, it hasn't been easy." Marie clasped her hands together. "There have been so many disappointed couples. Ally, you've been so understanding, and I really appreciate that, but most others haven't."

"I'm sorry to hear that." Ally scooted forward on the couch. "All I can think about is Vinnie's death, and you and your husband losing your business. It's such a terrible thing to happen."

"Thank you for your sympathy." Marie pushed a plate of cookies closer to them both. "But we'll be fine. We had insurance of course, on the barn."

"Oh, that's a relief to hear!" Charlotte smacked one hand against her knee. "How long do you think it will take to rebuild?"

"Actually, I don't think we will. The insurance pays out either way, and we could use the money to invest further in the farm, or set aside for retirement. Blake sank so much cash into that barn, but luckily he also made sure it was insured for its worth. Now that it has burned down, I think we're ready for a new chapter in our lives."

"I don't understand." Ally frowned as she searched the woman's eyes. "Blake seemed so upset about the fire, as if he would lose everything. Why wouldn't you want to rebuild?"

"He might have been upset in the moment, it was a scary experience. He probably felt some panic. But the truth is, he's been complaining to me about doing the weddings for a long time. It's a wonderful opportunity, and being part of every bride's special day is always a priceless experience, but it's also a ton of work." Marie sighed, then laughed. "I have to admit, I think a small part of him is relieved to have the pressure off his shoulders."

"That's good then." Charlotte nodded. "No one should be stuck doing something that they don't enjoy."

"Exactly, that's what I told him long before this happened. But he kept saying that he'd invested too much, and he had to get his money back out of it before he could stop doing the weddings. Our lives are certain to be a bit calmer." Marie picked up her mug and took a sip. "Aside from the death, of course. Blake is quite broken up about that, as am I."

"The murder." Ally watched the woman's reaction as she spoke the words. "It wasn't just a death, it was a murder, and arson. I'm surprised the insurance company is so willing to pay out, with criminal activity in play."

"It is still pending, but of course all of that will get sorted out when the killer is caught. That shouldn't take too long." Marie took another sip of coffee. "In order for the insurance not to pay out, Blake or I would have had to be responsible for the destruction of the barn, and obviously neither of us were. We were together all morning, until he went outside and smelled the smoke in the air."

"Did he leave right away to investigate?" Ally held her gaze. "Had he been inside with you before he smelled the smoke?"

"Yes, he went out to grab something from his truck, and then he shouted to me in the house, that he was going to go check out the smell." Marie shrugged. "I figured it was one of the neighbors having a bonfire or something, but he seemed a bit spooked. For good reason, it turns out." She shivered. "The idea that a murderer was on our property, and we had no idea, it's just disturbing."

"I'm sure it is." Charlotte reached across the table and patted her hand. "I'm sorry you're faced with all of this difficulty."

"It's temporary." Marie smiled. "That's what I keep telling myself. Soon enough Blake and I will be off on a tropical cruise somewhere, if I can convince him to go."

"That sounds like a nice plan." Charlotte nodded. "You said, not everyone has been as understanding as Ally. Have you had trouble with any of the other couples?"

"Oh, with wedding plans, comes nothing but trouble, trust me. Not you of course, Ally. You and Luke were a dream to work with. But in most cases, people are so emotional, and they want absolute perfection. If one thing goes wrong, or isn't exactly as requested, we're faced with a huge meltdown." Marie rolled her eyes. "It's too much sometimes. I'll be glad not to have to deal with that again. With the insurance money, we'll be able to refund the deposits everyone made and we can be done with all of this."

"Has Blake had any trouble with a couple recently? Before the fire?" Ally began to form a theory in her mind as she awaited Marie's response.

"Well." Marie winced as she looked down at the plate of cookies. "We did run into a bit of a bump in the plans for Vinnie and Becca's wedding. They wanted to have live doves released after the ceremony. Only we don't have a permit for that." She shrugged. "Blake had to tell him that he couldn't do it, unless they postponed the wedding long enough to get the permit. Vinnie didn't like that answer. I think he was used to getting what he wanted. Anyway, he insisted, and actually offered to pay more money. But Blake refused. He could have gotten into big trouble if he did it, and he likes to do things by the rules." She shook her head. "Vinnie was so angry, I thought he might cancel the wedding altogether. But I guess after he talked to Becca about it, he dropped the issue."

"And when did Blake and Vinnie argue about this?" Charlotte raised an eyebrow.

"I wouldn't call it an argument exactly. But it was a few days ago." Marie looked between them. "I'd appreciate it if you didn't mention it to the police, as it didn't mean anything. It was just a silly wedding issue, and I think they might take it the wrong way."

She frowned as she looked at Ally. "You understand, don't you?"

"Of course I do." Ally forced a smile. "Did anyone come around here asking about Vinnie? Anyone you didn't know?"

"No." Marie shook her head. "We haven't had too many people, other than the couples who planned to get married out here. Oh, the other day the electrician, Allan, came to install a couple of extra lights in the barn. Oh, and earlier that day Gloria the florist was out here to take some measurements for some arrangements. Actually, that was the same day that Blake and Vinnie discussed the birds. I remember because Blake was irritated that Vinnie lost his cool with someone else nearby. It just doesn't make things look very professional."

"I can see why he would be frustrated." Ally nodded. "I much prefer an unhappy customer talk with me privately to work things out, instead of in the middle of the shop."

"What problem could any of your customers have?" Marie grinned. "With those delicious chocolates you sell, everyone in this town loves you, and you too of course, Charlotte!"

"I'm glad you feel that way." Charlotte reached into her purse and pulled out a small box of candy.

"We brought these for you. A small thank you, for helping us along the way with the wedding."

"Oh, how sweet, in more ways than one!" Marie laughed as she took the box. "Thank you so much."

"Good luck to you, Marie, I hope things work out quickly for you." Ally stood up from the couch.

"Thank you, I have no doubt they will." Marie walked them to the door. "With Luke on the case, I'm sure he'll have the killer behind bars in no time."

"Me too." Ally smiled at her, then headed down the driveway toward her car.

As soon as her grandmother pulled the driver's side door shut, Ally looked over at her.

"An argument with Vinnie?"

"A motive for the fire?" Charlotte looked back at her. "I think our visit has stirred up plenty of new information."

"Why would he have acted upset about losing everything if he knew that he had insurance to cover it all?" Ally buckled her seat belt. "Something isn't right."

"Do you want to go by the station and talk with Luke?" Charlotte started the car.

"No, I want to speak to Gloria first. If she was there the day that Vinnie and Blake had their discussion about the doves, then maybe she can tell us just how intense of an argument it was."

"Do you really think Blake could have done this? Maybe Vinnie arrived at the barn early to discuss the birds again, and things got out of hand? If Blake killed him, and then set fire to the barn to cover it up, it would explain everything." Charlotte drove in the direction of the florist.

"It's possible, of course." Ally sighed. "But murdering someone over birds? It just seems like an extreme reaction."

"But if Vinnie is involved in criminal activity like Luke suspects, then maybe he went so far as to threaten Blake." Charlotte shook her head. "We can't rule it out. If Blake was as unhappy with doing the weddings as Marie claims, then maybe he just snapped."

"It's definitely something to look into more. Hopefully, Gloria can give us an idea of what she saw while she was out there."

CHAPTER 10

*C*harlotte pulled into a parking spot in front of the florist, and they stepped out of the car.

As Ally looked through the large front window she noticed Gloria alone in the shop. "It looks like a good time." She held open the door for her grandmother.

"Ally!" Gloria smiled as they stepped inside. "I was just about to call you."

"Hi Gloria." Ally took a breath of the various scents in the shop.

"I'm just wondering when you would like to place a new order for flowers? Have you found a new venue for the wedding, yet? We can always change the arrangements to suit it." Gloria walked around the counter toward them. "Oh listen to me, I'm just bombarding you, and not even giving you the chance to talk. I'm so sorry about that. Are you alright?"

"I'm fine, thank you." Ally bit back her frustration at being asked about the wedding, yet again. She had already told Gloria she was going to postpone it. "I don't have any plans to go through with the wedding at this point. I'd rather find out what happened to Vinnie first."

"I guess that would make sense. I'm sure your lovely groom is occupied at the moment." Gloria frowned. "But still, at some point, life has to go on right? You don't want to delay your wedding forever."

"Definitely not. Luke and I will get married, and soon. I'm actually here to ask you a question about your recent trip out to Blake's barn." Ally met her eyes. "Do you remember being out there a few days ago?"

"Oh, I guess." Gloria frowned, then shook her head. "I go out there now and then to take measurements for different requests." Her eyes widened as she nodded. "Oh yes, I remember now. I wanted to make sure I had the right amount of flowers for your archway, so I went out to look things over."

"Do you remember Blake and Vinnie being there?" Charlotte leaned against the counter beside her.

"Yes. I didn't really notice them at first." Gloria picked up a notebook from the counter and flipped it open. "I just jotted down my notes."

"Did you overhear the two of them talking? Maybe arguing?" Ally's heart pounded as she recalled the archway she'd chosen for the wedding and how beautiful she expected it to look. She forced the thought from her mind and focused her attention on Gloria.

"Yes, the two were a bit annoyed at each other as I recall. Vinnie shouted something about not getting what he paid for, and Blake yelled back about him being too demanding." Gloria winced. "I hurried to my car after that. I didn't want to be nosy."

"You didn't hear Vinnie say anything else?" Charlotte looked into her eyes. "He didn't threaten Blake at all?"

"Not that I heard. But when I started to drive away, I did see Vinnie put his hands on Blake. He just kind of shoved Blake's shoulders. It knocked Blake back a step or two. I was surprised that Vinnie would do that because Blake was so much bigger than him." Gloria sighed. "But then Blake just walked away."

"He didn't push Vinnie back? Or shout at him again?" Ally raised an eyebrow.

"No, not that I saw." Gloria shook her head. "Sorry, I didn't see or hear anything else. You're not thinking that Blake had something to do with this, are you?" She took a sharp breath. "He would never do something like that!"

"No, we're just trying to find out more about what was happening in Vinnie's life at the time." Ally bit into her bottom lip. "We're trying to get an idea of the kind of man Vinnie was."

"Well, I might not be able to tell you that, but I can tell you a little bit about the kind of man who came into my shop looking for Vinnie."

"Someone came into the shop looking for Vinnie?" Ally looked up at the corner of the ceiling closest to the register. "You don't happen to have cameras do you?"

"No, I've never felt I needed them in a place as quaint as this." Gloria placed her hands on her hips. "I guess I was wrong about that."

"That's alright. I'm sure that you got a good look

at him, right?" Charlotte surveyed the ceiling as well. "You have great lighting in here."

"Oh yes, I got a very good look at him. He was tall, and muscular. He had one of those wide chests." Gloria held her hands out, wide apart from each other. "Very muscular. He spoke to me rather softly at first. He complimented some flowers, and I suggested that he purchase some for his wife. He told me, he wasn't married. That's when he asked me about Vinnie."

"What did he say?" Ally took a slight step forward.

"He said that a friend of his was getting married, and that he was wondering if he had ordered flowers from me." Gloria clasped her hands together and looked down at them. "I told him more than I should have, I think. I thought he was Vinnie's friend, so I did say that Vinnie had ordered flowers from me. Then he asked if he could have Vinnie's address, as he wanted to surprise him with a gift. That's when alarm bells went off in my head. If he was a friend of Vinnie's why wouldn't he know his address?" She pursed her lips, then shook her head. "I told him that information was confidential and I couldn't share it. He got a bit testy after that. His whole demeanor was intimidating. He told me that he had to find

Vinnie, it was very important." She winced. "He seemed so angry."

"Were you scared?" Ally frowned as she noticed the shiver in Gloria's voice.

"I don't handle confrontation well, I never have. But I felt even more determined not to give him the address. When I refused again, he asked me where he could buy a gas can." Gloria looked toward the window. "I directed him to the gas station of course. After that, he left."

"Did you see him go toward the gas station?" Ally looked out the window as well. She could just see the sign for the gas station.

"I was too flustered to even look. I was just glad that he left." Gloria squeezed her hands into fists. "Now, I wish I had reported it to the police, but at the time, it seemed silly to do so."

"You did the right thing by not giving him Vinnie's address." Charlotte met her eyes. "You were very brave not to. Did he ever threaten you?"

"No, not with words, anyway. But he was such a big man, and angry. I just wanted him to leave. I told Luke about it earlier today, when he came by to ask me some questions." Gloria frowned. "I hope he finds that man. I'd guess that he's the one who did this."

"I hope so, too." Ally nodded.

"Maybe then we can talk about your wedding again?" Gloria smiled at her.

"Yes, then." Ally turned toward the door. "Thanks for the information, Gloria." She hurried outside. When they reached the car she turned to her grandmother. "Maybe we should take a look around the barn again. I might have overlooked something, since the fire was raging, and Becca and her family arrived in the middle of it all. Of course then I had no idea that this would be a murder investigation either." She opened the car door. "Would you mind coming with me?"

"Not at all. I think it's a great idea. Maybe the barn is in shambles, but that doesn't mean that the murderer didn't leave some kind of clue." Charlotte settled in the driver's seat.

"I still can't quite shake the fact that Blake acted so devastated, when he knew that he had a great insurance policy on the barn."

"Something doesn't add up there. Then hearing Gloria describe the argument, makes it even stranger."

"It does, especially since she saw Vinnie shove Blake, and Blake just walked away. It makes it less likely that Blake just snapped and killed Vinnie out

MOCHA, MARRIAGE AND MURDER

of anger, if he was able to control himself then." Ally frowned as she buckled her seatbelt. "If he didn't kill Vinnie out of anger, then why would he? Yes, maybe he made a profit from burning down the barn, but how did it benefit him to murder Vinnie?"

"You're right, it doesn't make sense. At least, not yet. Maybe there was more between the two men than we realize." Charlotte started the car. "It seems we learn something new about Vinnie every time we look into him. He had quite a few secrets. This man that needed a gas can, is looking far more guilty than anyone else."

"But who is he? If he worked with Vinnie, wouldn't Becca know about him? I'm starting to think that Becca is more involved in this than we first assumed. She should be doing everything she can to find out who killed her future husband."

"That's the thing, Ally. It's easy to be on the outside of someone's grief, and say what we think they should be doing, how we think they should be acting, but the truth is, everyone deals with things differently. She could be so heartbroken that she can't think straight. It might be less about refusing to cooperate, and more about not being capable of helping." Charlotte turned down the long driveway toward the barn. "She may still be in shock."

"You're right." Ally shook her head. "I am judging her. It's not fair of me to do that. The truth is, even finding Vinnie's killer isn't going to fix anything. It won't bring him back."

"No, it won't. But it will at least give her some answers, which is better than spending a lifetime wondering." Charlotte looked through the windshield at the remains of the barn. "Should we give Blake a call to let him know we're here."

"I don't think so. Hopefully, he won't be anywhere near the barn. We might be able to just have a good look around without interruption. If we tell him we're here, he'll probably want to watch our every step, or even try to stop us."

"You're right, having some privacy would be helpful." Charlotte studied the burnt barn.

"Where is Vinnie's car?" Ally's eyes widened as she looked over at her grandmother. "How did he get to the barn without his car?"

"It would be a full day's walk, or more, from town." Charlotte stepped out of the car. "I doubt that he would decide to take that long of a stroll."

"No, there's no way he walked here. But that means that someone brought him here." Ally paused as she stared at the charred remains of the barn. "Or at least they brought his body here. I don't know if

Luke has found his car. If he hasn't, it means maybe he met someone somewhere? Somewhere that his car hasn't been noticed?"

"Maybe." Charlotte walked along the exterior of the barn. "What a shame, it was so very beautiful. I couldn't wait to see you—"

"Mee-Maw!" Ally sighed. "No wedding talk!"

"I'm sorry." Charlotte turned to look at Ally. "So, we know that someone likely brought him here. But we don't know why, or whether he was alive at the time. It doesn't make much sense that the killer would have brought his body to the barn, though. Why? Weren't there other places that the killer could dispose of the body?"

"I would assume so." Ally crossed her arms. "According to the medical examiner's estimate, it's possible that Vinnie had been dead for a few hours before he was found. So, maybe whoever brought him here, did so before the sun came up. That would explain why no one noticed activity out here."

"That and the vast distance from any prying eyes." Charlotte turned as she swept her gaze across the rolling farmland. "Other than some wild critters, I doubt we have any witnesses."

A burst of chirps drew Ally's attention to a small cage behind the barn. "Look at these birds, Mee-

Maw." Ally walked over to the cage with her grandmother following. "I didn't notice them here during the fire, I guess because they were behind the barn."

"At least they're okay." Charlotte crouched down and cooed at them. "Hey there, birdies, are you doing okay?"

They chirped back at her and flapped their wings.

"Poor things shouldn't be in a cage." Charlotte sighed as she straightened up.

"They must be the birds that Vinnie and Blake argued about. I guess he got them after all."

The sound of another engine drew Ally's attention. She watched as Luke's car pulled to a stop near hers.

CHAPTER 11

"*A*lly." Luke stepped out of his car and walked toward her. "What are you doing out here?"

"We just wanted to look things over, now that the smoke has cleared. I wanted to see how bad it was and if it triggered any memories that would help me sort out what happened." Ally gazed at him for a moment then turned to look back at the barn. "We found out about an argument between Blake and Vinnie a few days ago about doves. Did Blake tell you about it?"

"He mentioned it." Luke nodded. "I know the doves are behind the barn. We have contacted the relevant people to make sure they are cared for."

"Great." Charlotte smiled with relief.

"And what about Allan, the electrician, installing some extra light fittings in the barn?" Ally asked.

"Yes, I know about that. But Allan has gone on a last-minute vacation and I can't get hold of him. I'll keep trying. But it's a bit suspicious, if you ask me." Luke looked around the property. "Actually, I also came here to look things over." He stared at the barn for a moment, then looked over at her. "I wanted to see if it's possible we overlooked something, maybe something that indicates how Vinnie got here. We haven't found his car, yet."

"So far we haven't seen anything obvious." Charlotte swept her gaze over the dry dirt. "Unfortunately, there are so many tracks, I guess it would be hard to distinguish one from the other."

"Yes, our technicians aren't having much luck with that." Luke shook his head. "I spoke to some of Blake's neighbors and I managed to find out that the lights Blake saw on the road late at night was one of their kids coming home from a friend's house."

"So, that's a dead end." Ally sighed.

"The techs have figured out that gasoline was likely the accelerant used in the fire." Luke crouched down and picked up a piece of the charred wood. Unfortunately, that doesn't help us much, because gasoline is very difficult to trace."

"Gasoline." Ally narrowed her eyes. "Remember what Gloria said, Mee-Maw?" She glanced over at her.

"About the stranger?" Charlotte nodded. "She said he asked her where he could buy a gas can."

"Oh really?" Luke straightened up. "And what did she say?"

"She sent him off to the gas station." Charlotte snapped her fingers. "I bet they have cameras there. They might have him on tape buying the gas can."

"She said that she told you about him, though, did she?" Ally narrowed her eyes.

"Yes, she did, but she said more to you. She told me about the stranger being there and asking about Vinnie, but not about the gas can. We've found several on the property here, but of course they all have explanations for being here. If someone actually brought the gas can to the barn, that might just be the lead we need to get moving on this case." A smile spread across his lips as he nodded. "Give me a second to call it in, it'll take me much longer to get to the gas station than one of the other officers in town."

As Luke walked away with his phone, Ally turned her attention to her grandmother. "This could be it. Maybe the stranger paid with a credit card, and they'll be able to track him down."

"Maybe." Charlotte tipped her head back and forth. "But I've never known a murderer to use their credit card to purchase his weapons." She rubbed her hand along her cheek. "Then there's the question, why did he buy the gas can? Did he know in advance that he was going to kill Vinnie? Did he plan to burn the barn down ahead of time? And why didn't Gloria tell Luke about this? It all feels so chaotic to me."

"It does." Ally nodded. "Maybe she was too scared. You saw how frightened she was when she talked about the stranger. Or maybe it just slipped her mind. And who knows what goes on in the mind of a killer. If he's the same person who killed Vinnie's business partner, maybe he has a reason behind his madness, that only he would know about."

"Maybe." Charlotte nodded. "From the way everyone described him, the stranger is a big guy, he certainly would have no trouble overpowering Vinnie, with him being so small."

"I guess we'll have to hope that the cameras were rolling at the gas station." Ally looked over at Luke as he walked back toward them.

"I have a couple of guys going out to the gas station to check things out. I did get Vinnie's phone records from that day. He didn't make any calls out, but he did receive a few calls. From Becca, from Blake, and from the flower shop." Luke frowned. "Blake didn't mention anything to me about calling him that morning, and neither did Becca. I'm going to have to find out more about that. But from what I can tell, from the length of the calls, they likely weren't answered, or the conversations were very brief."

"Which means that Vinnie might not have been alive when they came in." Ally tapped her fingertips against her hip as she considered the possibilities.

"That's one explanation. But the time of death can't be pinned down." Luke frowned. "The fact that Blake and Becca both called him when he might have already been dead, also indicates maybe they weren't involved."

"What about the flower shop?" Charlotte crossed her arms.

"It must have been about the wedding. I'll talk to Gloria about it." Luke looked at Ally. "I better get going."

"Okay." Ally gave him a kiss on the cheek.

She watched him walk away and waved to him as

he turned his car around and headed down the driveway.

Charlotte wrapped her arm around Ally's shoulders.

"What are you thinking?"

"Someone brought Vinnie here, Mee-Maw." Ally turned to look at the barn. "Someone drove him to this place, where he was supposed to get married, and killed him, or at least drove him here to leave his dead body." She shook her head as she released a long breath. "It sure seems like it was planned, doesn't it?"

"It is looking that way." Charlotte crossed her arms as she stared at the burnt wood in piles on the ground. "But looks can be deceiving. If we are to assume that someone brought him here after they killed him or with the intention of killing him, then it does seem to make all of this a lot more personal."

"There is only one person that we know, who would know Vinnie best on a personal level." Ally met her grandmother's eyes. "We need to try speak to Becca again. She's the best person to tell us more about Vinnie, except maybe this stranger who is looking for him."

"You're right." Charlotte nodded. "Let's see if she can give us something to work with."

"What are you two doing out here?" Blake spoke up from a few feet behind them.

Ally whirled around to face him as he stepped off of the trail that led across the wide field. "Blake, you startled me!"

"It wasn't my intention." Blake chuckled as his eyes widened. "Imagine my surprise when I walk around on my own property and find two uninvited and unannounced guests."

"We were just leaving." Charlotte opened the door of the car.

"Without the courtesy of telling me why you were here in the first place?" Blake folded his arms over his dusty denim jacket and stared at Charlotte. "My wife told me that you had a talk with her. Again, without being invited."

"We did call this morning to ask if we could come over and she agreed." Charlotte met his gaze.

"We're just trying to help figure out what happened here." Ally tried to meet his eyes. His unwavering gaze on Charlotte left her unsettled. "Don't you want the same thing?"

"What I want is for my property to become my property again. Between the cops, the looky-loos, including you two, it might as well be a public park. I just want my privacy back, is that so much to ask?"

Blake dropped his arms to his sides. "I've told the police everything I know. They also know I was home with my wife all morning. So, if you're sniffing around me thinking I had something to do with this, then you're way off course."

"Of course we don't." Ally tried to keep her voice even. "We are just trying to work out what happened here. You did tell me that you lost everything in this fire." She gestured to the ruins. "However, according to Marie, you're actually going to profit from the loss. I'm just confused about what the reality is."

"The reality is the one with the documentation to back it up." Charlotte cleared her throat. "From what we understand you stood to profit from the fire. We also know that an eyewitness saw you have an argument with Vinnie not long before he was killed."

"Eyewitness?" Blake laughed. "What do you think this is? True crime? Are you two going to write a book about me?" He rolled his eyes. "I know you suspect me and you can believe whatever you want. There's no way you can prove I killed Vinnie or had anything to do with the fire, because I didn't." He glared at them both. "Yes, at first, I panicked. I didn't think about the insurance, I just thought about how much time and money I've wasted on creating the perfect wedding venue, just to have people fight me on every tiny detail. Can we get more light inside the barn? Can we have a balloon release? Can't you find a way to stop the rain from falling?"

"That's what Vinnie did, right? He fought with you about the birds he wanted to have at the wedding?" Charlotte raised an eyebrow. "He even shoved you. That had to infuriate you."

"Of course it did." Blake shrugged. "But it's not the first time a groom, or a father of the bride, has gotten rough with me. They think they have to prove how big and in charge they are, so they take it out on me. I'm used to it." He smirked as he looked between the two of them.

"But you got him the birds, didn't you?" Ally glanced back at the remains of the barn.

"I did." Blake rolled his eyes. "I managed to pull some strings. I figured give him everything he wanted and get him out of my life. I even tried to call him that morning to tell him that I got the birds, but he didn't answer."

"I'm surprised you would get the birds after he threatened you." Charlotte narrowed her eyes. "Weren't you angry?"

"I'm not some short-tempered idiot that would risk going to jail over the pleasure of throwing a punch or two. Like I said, you're way off course. The two of you are wasting your time. If I see you on my property again, I'm going to take the proper steps to ensure that you are legally charged for it." Blake settled his gaze on Ally. "Which I'm guessing wouldn't go over too well with your fiancé, would it?"

Ally's heart skipped a beat at the thought. She knew that it would be terrible for Luke to have to charge her for any crime, not to mention it would harm his reputation.

"We're just leaving, as I said." Charlotte tapped Ally's shoulder. "Let's go. There's nothing more to discuss." She looked back over at Blake. "I thought you would want this solved. There is a murderer who is roaming free. The murderer might even still be hiding on your property. Had you considered that? If we can wander so freely, then so can the person who took Vinnie's life and burned down your barn. I think you would want this solved as quickly as possible."

"Of course I do." Blake nodded. "But I need to protect myself."

"The best way to protect yourself is to do everything you can to help find the murderer." Charlotte grabbed Ally's hand and guided her toward the car.

Ally's heart pounded as she joined her grandmother in the car. She felt Blake's eyes on them as the car rolled back down the driveway.

"That man!" Charlotte's tense voice snapped through the car. "He's either a killer or completely coldhearted."

"Or, he's trying to protect himself." Ally looked in the rearview mirror just in time to see Blake crouch down and look at something in the ashes of the barn. "He has to know that his argument with Vinnie makes him an even stronger suspect in the eyes of the police, and the insurance payout doesn't make things look any better."

"He could have done it, Ally. His wife could easily be helping him fake his alibi. He could have picked Vinnie up, under the guise of discussing the birds, brought him out to the barn, and decided to solve two problems at once. Get rid of Vinnie, who embarrassed him in front of Gloria, and be rid of hosting weddings, while making enough of a profit so he and his wife will be able to get away and travel like they want to." Charlotte shrugged. "It's a genuine motive."

"It is. But—" Ally sighed. "But could he really have been so angry over a shove that he plotted to kill Vinnie? If so, why would he bother to get the birds? He didn't lose his temper with us, he made it clear he's had run-ins with other customers. What would be so different about the way that Vinnie behaved, that Blake just decided to kill him? If he wanted the insurance money, there were easier ways to get it. Murdering someone, certainly makes the fire look suspicious, which will only hold up his payout." She bit into her bottom lip. "No, I think we're missing something. We need more information about Vinnie. Becca needs to start talking."

"That's presuming that she knows anything, considering he apparently has no history."

CHAPTER 12

inutes later, at Vinnie's front door, Ally's stomach churned. As determined as she was to find out more information about Vinnie and why Becca didn't offer information about him, she knew she had to tread carefully. If Becca wasn't the murderer, she had certainly lost someone she loved.

Charlotte met Ally's eyes and nodded.

Ally took a deep breath, then knocked on the door.

The door swung open. Becca stared out at the two of them, then frowned as she gestured for them to step inside.

"I guess you didn't bring candy and flowers this time?"

"Not this time." Ally shook her head. "I will drop some candies off later if you want. We were hoping to talk to you about Vinnie."

"Of course you were. That's all anyone wants to talk about." Becca sank down onto the couch in the living room, where Cliff already sat.

"Cliff, it's good to see you again." Charlotte met his eyes.

"He's been here to support me through all of this." Becca sniffled.

"That's very good of you." Charlotte smiled at Cliff.

Ally nodded to him, then cleared her throat.

"I think you know that Vinnie wasn't as innocent as he claimed to be. He was hiding something, wasn't he, Becca?" She settled into the chair across from the couch, and focused her attention on her.

"What?" Becca stared at her.

"Vinnie, he had secrets." Ally raised an eyebrow. "I think they might be what got him killed. You haven't been very helpful with information about Vinnie, but that isn't because you don't want to help, is it? It's because, you don't have any information to help."

Cliff shifted on the couch beside her. "Just tell her, Becca."

"I don't have anything to say." Becca crossed her arms. "At least not to the police. They have nothing but questions, no answers. All I need to know is what happened to my Vinnie, instead of telling me that, they keep asking me about his past."

"That's because he doesn't have one." Charlotte watched Cliff for a moment, then looked over at Becca. "People without pasts, usually have a lot of secrets. Don't you think?"

"He was a good guy!" Becca sniffled.

"Here you are." Cliff picked up a box of tissues from the coffee table and handed it to her. "Look, you're upsetting her." He shot a frown toward Ally. "Why are you even here?"

"I don't want to upset her. As you know, I was supposed to get married at that farm." Ally clasped her hands together. "I guess, I just want to know what happened. I want to help find out the truth. I know it won't bring him back, but it will at least give you some answers."

"That's all I'm asking for." Becca nodded as she wiped at her eyes with the tissue. "Sometimes I get distracted, and I forget for a minute, and then it hits me, that Vinnie is gone." She took a sharp breath. "I just can't believe this happened to me, to us."

"You need to tell them." Cliff frowned. "They are going to find out eventually."

"Tell us what?" Ally's eyes widened.

"I did see him that morning," Becca whispered as she tugged at the edges of her tissue. The nervous movement caught Ally's attention. "Cliff had done some digging, and figured out that Vinnie was lying to me about his business. There was no explanation for his wealth. After I discovered that his business wasn't really a business, it had no offices, no history, I wanted to find out the truth about it, about him. I found him near the coffee shop he likes to get his morning coffee at, Coffee on Main, and I demanded to know the truth." She glanced up at Ally, then tugged at the tissue again. "He told me that he had some secrets. But that he loved me, and we could work through it."

"Did you believe him?" Ally waited for her to look up, then met her eyes. "Becca, didn't it make you angry that he had lied to you?"

"Of course it did." Becca tossed the tissue down in her lap and leaned her head back as she rolled her eyes. "I was furious! I thought I knew everything about him. I honestly thought that this was some kind of lie that Cliff made up to try to break us up.

When Vinnie admitted to lying to me, it was devastating."

"I would never lie to you, Becca." Cliff frowned. "Now, you know I was only trying to look out for you. You must know that, don't you?" He placed his hand over hers.

"I know that now, Cliff, and I can't thank you enough." Becca shook her head. "But to hear Vinnie admit to lying to me all that time. It broke my heart."

"That must have been so difficult. You must have been so angry." Charlotte nodded as she met Becca's eyes. "You expected to build a life with this man, and then you find out he lied to you? Of course you were angry! I couldn't blame you if you lost your temper. If you hurt him."

"No, I didn't. I was angry, yes." Becca stood up. "But don't twist my words! I didn't hurt him. I never touched him! I just left. I came back home. I have no idea where he went after that."

"Did anyone else see the two of you talking?" Ally stood up as well and stepped closer to her grandmother.

"I don't think so." Becca sank back down onto the couch as she shook her head. "I'm not sure. I wasn't paying attention to anything else. Honestly, I was losing my mind. But I didn't hurt Vinnie, I would never do that!" Her voice trembled as she picked the tissue up that had fallen to the floor. "I loved him, you know."

"You loved him, but didn't you think it was important to tell the police about this?" Ally's voice softened.

"And have them suspect me even more?" Becca's eyes widened as she shook her head. "I thought losing someone I loved would be the worst thing I've ever experienced. But it isn't. The worst thing is being accused of taking his life, not even being allowed to grieve my loss, because I am terrified I will end up behind bars."

"It's time for you to go." Cliff stood up and gestured to the door. "None of this is helping her."

Tanya stepped into the room from the hall, and frowned. "What is going on here?"

Ally bit into her bottom lip as she realized Cliff was right. Although Becca had admitted to seeing her future husband the morning of the fire, even that wouldn't solve the murder. However, it did make her a far more likely suspect.

"Just one last question, and then we'll be on our way." Ally glanced at Charlotte, then looked back at Becca. "Has a large muscular man with a mustache asked you about Vinnie?"

Tanya ducked back into the hallway.

"I can't talk about this anymore." Becca shook her head. "You need to leave."

"That's it, time to go." Cliff directed them both to the door.

~

Ally got into the car and sighed.

"Do you believe her?" Charlotte settled in the driver's seat.

"I'm not sure. We certainly know that she lied to Luke. She claimed not to have seen Vinnie that morning. Why would she lie about it? Why would she let the police wonder when Vinnie died, when she knew that he was alive that morning?" Ally looked at her grandmother. "This whole time she's been holding back that information."

"She's right about it making her look guilty. She may have just been too afraid to tell the truth." Charlotte started the car.

"But then why tell us about it just now?" Ally sighed. "It doesn't make any sense to me. None of it does. She claims she loves him, but she doesn't want to solve his murder. Doesn't that tell you that she's the one who killed him? What other possible explanation could there be?"

"Maybe someone else she loves did it?" Charlotte glanced over at her. "If it were her cousin, or her father, or even Cliff, she might feel the urge to protect them."

"She'd protect the person who murdered Vinnie?" Ally narrowed her eyes.

"Yes. Think it through, Ally." Charlotte turned the car onto the main road. "She's just lost someone, and then she's faced with the possibility of losing someone else she cares about. Whether she agrees with what they did or not, she may feel the need to protect them."

"Maybe." Ally shook her head. "But I don't know. It would still be her protecting her future husband's killer."

"Her future husband who lied to her." Charlotte shrugged. "Maybe she didn't love him as much as she claims."

"Maybe. Would you mind stopping at the florist? I want to ask Gloria about her call to Vinnie that morning. It probably won't lead to anything, but I want to speak to everyone who might have had contact with Vinnie that day." Ally looked out the window at the florist.

"Of course." Charlotte pulled the car into a parking spot. "While you do that I'll grab us some food. We didn't have any lunch and I'm starving."

"Great, thanks." Ally stepped out of the car and headed right into the florist.

Gloria gasped as she turned to face the door.

Ally detected the fear in her eyes before she gave a short laugh.

"Sorry Ally, you startled me." Gloria brushed her hair back behind her ear, then smiled. "It's been a busy day. Many people are rearranging their wedding plans."

"I bet it's been crazy." Ally noticed a pile of papers on the counter near the register. "Do you run this shop all by yourself?"

"Yes. During the holiday season I sometimes hire a helper or two, but mostly it's just me." Gloria shrugged. "I haven't been in business long, so I try to keep the costs down."

"I understand that." Ally stepped closer to the counter and tried to glance at the words on the top piece of paper without Gloria noticing. "Have you had anyone come in that was particularly upset?"

"Everyone is stressed, of course. But as far as upset, no I wouldn't say so. The wedding must go on, right? Even if there is a bump in the road, that joyful union has to happen."

"Do I notice a hint of sarcasm in your tone?" Ally smiled as she raised an eyebrow.

"Did you?" Gloria took a step back. "I'm sorry if you did. I'm just a little tired from trying to keep up with everything today. I have so many calls to make."

"I probably just heard you wrong." Ally gave up on trying to see the paper, and focused on the telephone behind the counter instead. "I guess you make a lot of calls to your customers?"

"I call to confirm orders every day. Usually a day or two before the orders are due to be delivered. It's just a good way to make sure that there are no surprises or last-minute changes needed." Gloria picked up the stack of papers and slid them into a drawer behind the counter. "It's a good way to keep up to speed with my customers, too. I like to check in with how they are doing."

"Did you happen to call Vinnie about the flowers on the morning of the fire?" Ally met Gloria's eyes.

"Oh yes." Gloria frowned. "Yes, I did call him. To confirm some of the flowers for the wedding."

"Did you talk to him?" Ally leaned forward slightly.

"Yes, I did. He confirmed the order. That was all."

Gloria shrugged. "It's difficult to think that I might have been one of the last people to speak with him."

"Did you tell the police about this?" Ally's heart skipped a beat.

"Oh, no, I didn't think to mention it." Gloria shook her head. "It doesn't seem very important."

"Are you kidding? Not important?" Ally stared straight into her eyes. "All information about that morning is important. You speaking to Vinnie that morning confirms that he was alive, it makes the window of when he may have been killed much smaller."

"I didn't think of that." Gloria frowned.

"You need to tell the police right away that you spoke to him, and exactly what he said." Ally pulled out her phone and started a text to Luke.

"No, I'd rather not get involved." Gloria shook her head. "It's not my place."

"Gloria, it's terribly important." Ally sent the text, then looked up at Gloria again. "Don't you want to help the police figure out what happened to Vinnie?"

"I thought they already had a suspect. That guy that was looking for him?" Gloria shook her head. "I'm so confused. Isn't that the case?"

"They haven't been able to find that man yet. It may have just been a coincidence that he showed up looking for Vinnie around the time that Vinnie was killed. Gloria, can you tell me exactly what Vinnie said to you when you spoke to him?" Ally stepped closer.

"Exactly? No, I don't think so." Gloria sighed. "I was busy, you know, hurrying to make the calls. I don't think I can remember exactly what he said. I make so many calls. I'm sure he just confirmed the order."

"But you don't remember if he did or not?" Ally narrowed her eyes.

"Uh, let me check." Gloria pulled a notebook from a shelf and opened it up. As she skimmed through a handwritten list in the notebook, she clucked her tongue. She poked her finger at one entry, then nodded. "I have a check mark beside his name for that day. That means that he confirmed it."

"Any questions you've had so far about my upcoming wedding, you have always called me to talk about it. Is there a reason you called Vinnie instead of Becca?" Ally met her eyes.

"Oh, I tried to call Becca, but she didn't answer. I needed final confirmation before I could move forward with last-minute additions to the order, so I called Vinnie and he answered." Gloria shrugged. "I guess I was so busy I didn't really think about it until now."

"Did you hear anything in the background of the call? Did it sound like someone else was with him?" Ally's heart skipped a beat as she hoped for a tiny detail that would turn into a break in the case.

"No, I can't say that I did. Like I said, it was just a quick conversation." Gloria glanced up at the clock. "And as I also mentioned, I do have a lot to get done today."

"Of course. I'll let Luke know about your conversation." Ally was sure he would want to speak to Gloria about it. He already knew she had called Vinnie on the morning of the fire.

"Great." Gloria picked up the store phone and turned away as she began to dial it.

CHAPTER 13

*lly stepped out of the florist and spotted her grandmother with two sacks of food.

"Well?" Charlotte handed her one of the bags. "Anything?"

"Only that Gloria spoke to Vinnie that morning, and she didn't think to tell the police about it." Ally rummaged in the bag for a french fry, then frowned. "How could she not think to tell the police?"

"Maybe with everything going on it just slipped her mind. Why don't we take our food back to the cottage and eat with Arnold and Peaches?" Charlotte smiled. "I'm sure Arnold would appreciate a few of these fries."

"That sounds great. But I'll have to save some for him, I'll have to go a bit later. I have a few more orders I need to fill today." Ally glanced in the direction of the shop. "But you can take a break."

"Nonsense, I'll join you. We can get the orders done together."

"I really appreciate that, Mee-Maw, but you've done enough to help already. I can handle them, it's just a few orders. Maybe you can give Mrs. Bing a call and see if she knows of anyone that might have seen Vinnie and Becca together outside that coffee shop. I'd love to be able to confirm her story." Ally started to cross the street.

"Ally, wait." Charlotte grabbed her wrist and tugged her closer as her gaze locked on a man across the street from them.

"What is it, Mee-Maw?" Ally looked across the street for what might have spooked her. Her eyes settled on a man, who lingered just outside the door of the ice cream shop. Instead of going inside, he held up a photograph to the people that walked past. "Do you think that's him?" She gasped.

"If it is, what is he doing here?" Charlotte narrowed her eyes. "Do you think he's still looking for Vinnie?"

"Maybe." Ally took a step forward. "I'm going to find out."

"Ally, no." Charlotte's grip tightened on her wrist.

"We have no idea how dangerous this man might be. He could be responsible for two murders, that we know of, and maybe even more. We should just call Luke."

"But he's starting to walk away, Mee-Maw!" Ally twisted her wrist and pulled it free. "I promise I'll be careful. You call Luke, and keep an eye on me. I'll signal you if I think I'm in trouble."

"Ally!" Charlotte reached for her hand again.

Ally stepped out of reach and quickly crossed the street. She glanced back once to make sure that her grandmother wasn't following her. She could see that she was waiting on the other side of the road for a few cars to pass before she crossed. Ally turned her attention to the man a few feet ahead of her. As she quickened her pace to catch up to him, she wondered if her grandmother might have been right to urge caution. The large man became larger with every step she took closer to him.

Before she could get any closer, he opened the door to a car parked along the street, and got in. Within a few seconds he started it, and pulled away from the curb.

Ally did her best to memorize the license plate, then pulled out her phone and typed it out.

"Ally!" Charlotte caught up with her as the car roared down the street. "Did you speak to him?"

"No, he took off before I could." Ally shook her head. "I missed my chance."

"I told you not to go after him!"

"Mee-Maw, I would have been fine. If I got into trouble you would have helped me. You would have come to my rescue. I want to talk to him so this murder can be solved!"

"Luke can talk to him! The one with a badge, and a gun, remember?" Charlotte looked into her eyes.

"I'm sending him the plate number now. Hopefully, he will be able to catch up with him." Ally smiled.

"Hopefully."

"And you know you would have gone after him, just like I did." Ally nodded.

"No, I wouldn't have." Charlotte smiled slightly. "You have always been too brave for your own good."

"Brave?" Ally laughed, then shook her head. "If I had been brave, I would have tackled him!"

"Nonsense!" Charlotte laughed as her phone beeped with a text. She quickly read it.

"I'm going to go finish up those orders at the

shop." Ally smiled. "Nothing dangerous about that right? That's all I'm going to do."

"Promise?" Charlotte looked into her eyes.

"I promise."

"Alright then, I just got a text from Jeff, he has a few hours free. He's just at the park down the road. I'll go meet him there and we can check on Peaches and Arnold for you. Then I'm going to track down Mrs. Bing, Mrs. Cale, and Mrs. White, to see if they can shed some light on Becca's story."

"Keep me up to date." Ally waved to her, then walked toward the chocolate shop. As she did, she searched the streets for any sign of the stranger's car. Although she had promised she would just make candy, she knew if the opportunity presented itself she would try to speak to the man again. And she knew if her grandmother was in the same position she would do the same. Charlotte was actually much braver than Ally and more stubborn, if that was possible. Ally wished she'd been brave enough to speak up and demand his attention before he'd left.

As Ally worked on the last box of candies she needed to fill, the bell over the door of the shop rang. She realized she hadn't locked it. Even though they were closed she still looked up with a smile, eager for a customer to distract her from the thoughts of the murder that swirled through her mind.

Ally's smile vanished as her breath caught in her throat.

The large man with the mustache walked toward the counter, his eyes locked to hers.

"Have you seen this man?" He held up a picture as he stared at Ally. "His name is Vinnie, and I'm trying to find him."

"That man?" Ally's heart pounded as she looked into Vinnie's eyes in the photograph. When the picture had been taken, he was still alive, he had no idea how his life would eventually end. She bit into her bottom lip.

"Yes, this man." He narrowed his eyes as he leaned closer. "Is something wrong? Is there something you don't want to tell me? I need all of the information that you have on him."

"Let me think about it for a second." Ally picked up her phone. "If I remember correctly I might have seen him earlier."

"Where?" His tone sharpened.

"Just one second." As Ally tried to type out a message to Luke, her fingertips struck the wrong letters. Her hand trembled as she sent the jumbled message, then she looked back up at the man. "What was your name again?"

"I didn't give you my name. I'm asking for information from you, not the other way around." He chuckled, then straightened up. He picked up a wooden race car and spun the wooden wheels across his palm. "Beautiful craftsmanship. It's fascinating how people can still make things of beauty, when we live in a world of mass manufacturing, isn't it?" He spun the wheels again. "Now, where did you see him?"

"I'm not sure exactly. It might have been at the grocery store." Ally shrugged. "I see him around now and then. I can give him a message for you, if you'd like."

"No, that won't be necessary." He sighed, then picked up one of the sample chocolates. "I suppose while I'm here I should buy something. Do you have a small, assorted pack?"

"Sure, I can get you one." Ally edged toward the shelf behind the register. She didn't dare to take her eyes off of the man as she grabbed one of the boxes on the shelf, then placed it on the counter. "That'll be twelve dollars."

"Expensive candy." He winced, then placed the candy he held into his mouth. "Oh, yes, I see. It's worth the price." He smiled as he ate the cherry cordial.

"Are you just in town to visit your friend?" Ally slipped the box into a bag.

"He's not my friend." He looked into her eyes again. "He's a very dangerous man. If you see him, you should contact me." He pulled a twenty dollar bill out of his wallet, then followed it with a business card with just a phone number on it. "Anytime, day or night, the moment you lay eyes on him. Understand?"

"Dangerous how?" Ally narrowed her eyes as she dug into the register for his change.

"If you see him, you let me know." He took his change as he held her gaze.

"How about first you tell me what you think he did that's so terrible." Ally walked around the counter as he turned toward the door.

"I'm the one asking questions here." He turned back to face her. "Like, why were you following me earlier?"

Ally's muscles tensed as she stared at him. He'd known she was following him? Was that why he'd shown up at the shop not long after?

"I've been looking for you." Ally cleared her throat. "To ask you some questions."

"Me?" His gaze sharpened as he stared at her. "Why?"

"Why are you looking for Vinnie?" Ally moved closer to him, determined to prevent him from leaving. She could only hope that Luke understood her jumbled message and was on his way. Until then, she wanted to keep the stranger talking.

"That's my business." He turned toward the door again.

Ally stepped in front of him and blocked the doorway. "Maybe you'd like to know what I know about Vinnie then."

"Yes, I would." He crossed his arms. "I think I've made that clear."

"He's dead. Someone murdered him on Wednesday morning." Ally studied every twitch of his facial muscles.

Shock briefly took over his expression before he looked away. "The fire I heard about? He was in it?"

"He was killed, and it's believed someone then set the fire to try to cover up his murder." Ally closed her hand over the doorknob behind her and stared straight at him. "You wouldn't know anything about that, would you?"

"Me?" He glared at her. "No, obviously I didn't

know anything about that, otherwise I wouldn't still be looking for him."

"Unless, you wanted to make it seem like you didn't know he was dead." Ally shrugged. "What better alibi than pretending to be ignorant?"

"Let me pass. I have nothing else to say to you." He stepped closer to her.

"No, you're not going anywhere." Ally tightened her grip on the doorknob.

"Move aside." His thick, heavy hand landed on her shoulder with just enough pressure to guide her away from the door.

Ally tightened her muscles and remained where she stood.

"Not until you speak to the police."

"The police?" He scowled at her. "What did you do?" His hand tightened around her shoulder.

The doorknob jerked in her hand.

"Ally! Open the door!"

Ally stepped aside as Luke pushed the door open.

"There he is, Luke!" She pointed straight at the man who stumbled back a few steps. "He's the one who has been looking for Vinnie!"

"I was just leaving." The man held up his hands. "I don't want any trouble."

"Then you'll be happy to answer a few of my

questions? I'm Detective Luke Elm with the Blue River Police Department." Luke held up his badge and stepped between Ally and the man. "Why don't we start with your name?"

"It's Joe." He sighed as he lowered his hands. "Joe Haversfield."

"How do you know Vinnie, Joe?" Luke shifted to the side to block the door as Joe stepped toward it.

"His name wasn't Vinnie to begin with." Joe sighed. "He's a conman, and he's had many different names. He stole people's identities."

CHAPTER 14

"*A*conman?" Luke frowned as he stared at Joe. "We already know he's into some kind of illegal business. But what makes you think he's a conman?"

"It's not any kind of business. He's a thief. He cons people, takes every dime he can from them. Disappears and changes his name." Joe held up his hands again. "If you let me reach into my pocket, I can show you some of the pictures I have on my phone of his previous identities."

"Go on." Luke nodded, and moved closer to Ally again.

"That doesn't explain who you are." Ally watched as Joe showed Luke some pictures on his phone.

"I'm someone who wanted to stop him from

doing it again." Joe frowned. "But apparently someone already did."

"Is that what you consider murder?" Luke narrowed his eyes. "Stopping someone?"

"I don't consider it anything." Joe's tone hardened. "I had nothing to do with any of it."

"Maybe you'd like to tell me about your whereabouts on Wednesday morning?" Luke asked.

"I don't have to tell you anything. I'm leaving." Joe brushed past Luke as he headed through the door.

"Sir, your cooperation would go a long way. I have a few questions for you."

"Not saying another word!" Joe shouted back over his shoulder, then headed for his car.

"Luke, are you really going to let him go?" Ally watched as the door swung shut behind Joe.

"There's nothing I can do at the moment, Ally." Luke frowned. "I checked the cameras at the gas station. There's no evidence that he ever bought a gas can from there. In fact, the clerk working that day doesn't recall selling one to anyone. He hasn't committed a crime." He looked over at her. "Not one we can prove yet, at least."

"I understand. But I just can't shake the idea that he must have had something to do with this. I understand why people described him as seedy. He has such a dangerous energy to him."

"Which is exactly why I don't want you pursuing this any further." Luke took her hands and turned her to face him. "Can I trust you to stay away from this guy?"

"But Luke, he could be the key to solving Vinnie's murder." Ally pursed her lips.

"Which is exactly why I'm going to investigate him." Luke searched her eyes. "You need to stay out of this. I need some time to figure out how he fits into all of this. Okay?" He held her gaze. "Promise me?"

Ally's muscles tensed as she resisted the urge to argue the point. She could tell from the stern expression on Luke's face that he wouldn't budge, and she had to admit that he might be right not to. Though she hated to admit it, the memory of being alone with Joe left her as unsettled as Luke seemed to be.

"I promise, I won't go after him. But he's the one who came in here. Remember?" Ally raised an eyebrow.

"You need to let me know if he comes near you again. It makes me uneasy that he sought you out in particular to ask about Vinnie. With you and

Charlotte going around town asking questions, he might already suspect that you're on to him. His whole visit here might have just been to intimidate you. You need to be careful."

Ally winced as she recalled her attempt to chase him down earlier that afternoon and Joe's comments about her following him.

"I'll be careful, Luke, I promise." She leaned close and kissed his cheek.

"I'll try catch up with you later." Luke released her hands and started toward the door.

Ally closed her eyes as the door swung shut. Her head throbbed with a mixture of fear and frustration. When the bell over the door chimed again, her entire body jolted in reaction to the sound.

She was relieved to see her grandmother come through the door, followed by Jeff.

Ally hugged Charlotte and greeted Jeff. She quickly explained what had happened with Joe.

"Ally, are you okay?" Charlotte cupped her cheeks as she looked into her eyes. "It must have been scary to be alone with him."

"Honestly, it was a little." Ally grasped her grandmother's hands and squeezed them as she pulled them from her cheeks. "But I'm okay, I promise. With this new information, though, the possibilities have really split wide open."

"You're right. We suspected that Vinnie was up to something illegal, but being a con artist changes everything. Any number of his victims could be trying to seek revenge on him. Past partners in crime could be after him, too. We still don't know which Joe is." Charlotte frowned. "My guess is, if he was looking for Vinnie, he might be someone he worked with before."

"Which means he's likely a con artist, too." Ally narrowed her eyes. "I don't believe that he didn't know that Vinnie was already dead. What I'm not sure of, is why is he still here asking questions about Vinnie if he's the one who killed him?"

"That's a good question. Maybe he thinks it makes him look innocent?" Charlotte shrugged. "If that's the case, then he may have decided to stick around and keep asking questions, so the police wouldn't suspect him as the killer."

"It's possible. It sounds like a con artist's way of thinking." Ally raised an eyebrow. "The only way that Luke can arrest him though, is if we find some evidence. We're going to have to do some serious digging to find anything. We have very little to start with. All we have is his name."

"And the fact that he seems to be pretty confident about Vinnie being a con artist." Charlotte frowned. "This changes things quite a bit. If he really was conning Becca, then her motive has grown, as have her father and cousin's."

"Don't forget Cliff." Ally crossed her arms. "If he wanted to protect Becca, he might have decided to get rid of Vinnie. Think about it, if Cliff found out that Becca hadn't broken up with Vinnie even after she found out he'd been lying to her about his business, maybe he felt he had to take things a step further."

"That's a good point." Charlotte nodded. "He might have been furious that she still would choose a liar over him. I think he has plenty of motive as well. Maybe we should talk to them again?"

"I definitely think we should. But it's getting late tonight. I'm going to close up and go home for the night. If I can find out some more information about Joe, that would be great. Until then, I'm going to hope that Luke turns something up."

"Alright." Charlotte hugged her. "Do you want some help cleaning up?"

"No, I'll be fine. There isn't much to do. Thanks Mee-Maw." Ally looked into her grandmother's eyes. She'd tried to warn her not to go after Joe, but Ally hadn't listened. What if he showed up to intimidate her next? She needed to make sure that didn't happen. "Let's both get a fresh start in the morning, alright?"

"Yes, that sounds good. I'll spend some time with Jeff." Charlotte gave her one more quick hug.

"Be careful when you leave, alright?" Jeff looked over at Ally.

"Don't worry. I don't think Joe will be coming anywhere near me again, Luke made sure of that. I won't be much longer."

"Okay, the shop is closed for a couple of days, so I'll come by the cottage in the morning?" Charlotte smiled. "Jeff can drop me off."

"Great. Have a good night."

After her grandmother and Jeff left, Ally took some time to organize a few of the shelves in the kitchen, then grabbed the broom to sweep up the front of the shop. She locked everything up and headed to her car.

On her way to the car, Ally remembered that she hadn't told Luke about her conversation with Becca. She ignored her wave of tiredness and went back into the shop to get him some candies and a coffee. Hopefully, she would find him at the station and she knew he would appreciate a snack.

Ally drove the short distance to the police station. Her heart raced as she entered the building. Maybe Luke had found something? Maybe when he saw her he would want to discuss her run-in with Joe further? She hadn't exactly told him everything about their encounter. Luke didn't know that she had actually followed him first.

"Ally!" Luke waved to her from his office and stood up as she walked in. "This is a nice surprise." He closed the door behind her.

"I wanted to drop these off." Ally handed him the candy and coffee. "I hope I'm not disturbing you."

"Thank you." Luke smiled. "I have a few minutes."

"I also want to tell you something. I meant to tell you earlier but I got distracted by Joe." Ally sat down in the chair in front of his desk. "About Becca."

"What about her?" Luke met her eyes as he sat down as well.

"She talked with Vinnie in person the morning he was killed." Ally frowned.

"She spoke to him?" Luke's voice tightened as he stared across the desk at her.

"Yes, at Coffee on Main. I meant to tell you as soon as I found out, but it's been such a crazy day. I don't know if she will tell you the same thing, but she told me that she spoke to Vinnie that morning after her ex-boyfriend Cliff told her about the information he found about his business. Or non-existent business. She insisted that she didn't have anything to do with his death." Ally sighed as she scooted her chair closer. "But what I can't figure out, is if she didn't kill him, why didn't she tell you about speaking to him?"

"From the first moment I spoke to her, she claimed that she hadn't seen him that morning." Luke sat back in his chair and folded his hands behind his head. "It could be that she lied to protect herself, or it could be that she lied to protect someone else." He sat up again and met her eyes. "You said that it was the ex that told her the truth about Vinnie's business, right?"

"Yes. He was with her when Mee-Maw and I spoke with her." Ally quirked an eyebrow. "Do you think he could have had something to do with this?"

"I think it's possible. Maybe he's still in love with her, and that's why he did the digging in the first place. Maybe he decided that he was going to break the two of them up, and that's why he told her about the business. But maybe that wasn't enough for him, and he decided to eliminate the competition altogether. He could have killed Vinnie after Becca spoke to him."

"And she found out, and wanted to protect him?" Ally shivered. "Do you really think she could go from wanting to marry Vinnie to wanting to protect his killer that fast?"

"I'm not sure what to think. Clearly, she's okay with lying to the police." Luke looked down at the file on his desk. "The only problem with my theory is that the ex has an alibi for the time of the murder. He was at work, and his boss confirmed that he had clocked in that morning. The alibi didn't eliminate him completely when Vinnie's time of death was a wider window, but now that we know we're down to about a two hour window, it does confirm his alibi."

"Did his boss actually see him there? Or did he just have a computerized record of him clocking in?" Ally shrugged. "Maybe he showed up to work, clocked in to create an alibi, then went off to murder Vinnie."

"It's possible." Luke scratched his cheek, then nodded. "I'll double check and see if we can get any visual evidence that he was there, or if anyone else can confirm his presence." Luke glanced up at her. "Maybe, even after telling Becca about this, she still planned to marry Vinnie, and that was enough to send Cliff into a jealous rage."

"Maybe." Ally stood up from the chair. "But why at the barn?"

"Yes, why at the barn?" Luke looked back down at the file. "There are still plenty of pieces that need to be fit together. But I'm definitely going to have another conversation with Becca, and with Cliff." He looked up at her. "Thank you for the information, Ally."

"Of course." Ally began to pace back and forth in front of the desk. "By the way, when I asked Becca about seeing a large man with a mustache she avoided the question. She ended our conversation."

"When I spoke to her earlier, I also asked her about him. She insisted that she didn't know who he was. My instincts told me then that she wasn't lying, but it's pretty clear my instincts have been off." Luke sighed as he stared at her. "I've been a little distracted."

"Distracted by?" Ally met his eyes.

"Never mind. I'd better get on this." Luke picked up his phone. "I've got some calls to make."

"I'll see if I manage to find out anything else about Joe." Ally paused in the doorway. "You know I have my sources."

"Yes, I do." Luke smiled as he dialed the phone.

"Let me know what Mrs. Bing, Mrs. Cale and Mrs. White have to say." He winked at her.

Ally smiled as she closed the door behind her. She loved that even though the three tended to cause a bit of drama around town, he seemed to love them as much as she did.

CHAPTER 15

*A*fter the short drive home, Ally unlocked the door to the cottage and stepped inside.

Arnold trotted up to her, eager for pets and treats.

A lump of orange fur on the back of the couch indicated that Peaches couldn't be bothered with her. She knew why. Peaches could get a little cranky when she was left at home alone with Arnold for too long. Although, the adventurous cat liked Arnold's company, and they would get up to mischief together, she would get bored with him after a while. She missed the company of humans.

"Peaches, don't pout." Ally offered her a few treats after giving some to Arnold. "I know it's been a long day."

Peaches picked each treat off of Ally's palm with a delicate bite that barely grazed her skin.

Ally smiled as she looked into her eyes. "You know I would never stay away too long, precious."

Peaches meowed, then stretched her long body and yawned.

"Oh, I bore you, do I?" Ally laughed, then flopped down on the couch. "A lot has happened today." Her mind spun with thoughts of the murder.

Peaches jumped down onto the couch beside her. Arnold lay on the floor by Ally's feet.

Ally feathered her fingers through the cat's fur and closed her eyes. "Oh Peaches, I am so happy to be home with you."

Peaches purred and curled up in her lap.

"I wish the murder was solved. Instead, I have no idea who killed Vinnie."

Peaches pawed at her arm and met her eyes.

"Okay fine, maybe I have some idea. But I don't have any proof, do I?" Ally frowned as she stroked under the cat's chin. "I know there's something I'm missing, Peaches. Did Becca find out he was a conman and killed him? Could Cliff be so in love with her, that he decided to eliminate his competition? I just don't know anymore." She frowned. "Then there's Joe. Joe, who is a perfectly good suspect, but that's part of the problem. He's too good of a suspect. He claimed he was here because he wanted to stop Vinnie. If so, why didn't he go to Becca? Why didn't he turn Vinnie in to the police?" She shook her head, then closed her eyes. "I do hope all of this will be a bit clearer in the morning."

As Ally began to drift off to sleep, her thoughts filled with memories of the flames that leapt out of the barn. She remembered the sensation of Luke's arms around her, pulling her away from the collapsing structure.

Then her thoughts shifted to her delayed wedding. She wanted to be with Luke, not just as his fiancée, but as his wife. Was that how Becca felt when Vinnie confessed to his illegal business dealings? Had she been willing to forgive him for absolutely anything?

The sound of a loud snort made Ally's eyes fly open.

Confused, Ally stared at the ceiling, while Arnold nudged her cheek with his snout. As she realized she'd fallen asleep on the couch with Peaches still curled up beside her, her pounding heart began to settle.

"Good morning, Arnold." Ally smiled as she stroked the top of the pig's head. "You're the best alarm clock ever, you know that?"

As Ally sat up on the couch she knew exactly where she had to go to find the answers she needed. After sending a text to her grandmother to explain what she was up to, she took a quick shower, fed the pets and played with them for a bit, then grabbed a banana on her way out the door, and headed straight for Vinnie's house. She wanted to speak to Becca.

When Ally neared the house she decided to park a short distance away. If Becca was aware of her approach, she might come up with a reason to turn her away. She walked from her car toward Vinnie's house, which allowed her a view of the rear of the house. As she looked around, the back door of the house swung open and Tanya stepped outside.

"Ally." She froze near the door. "What are you doing back here?"

Ally's heart pounded as she realized there was no good excuse for her to be there.

"My cat." She took a sharp breath. "She's gone missing, and she loves to wander. I thought I saw her come back here."

"Your cat?" Tanya stared at her. "Your story is

that your cat came all the way to Mainbry and just happened to wander into Vinnie's backyard?"

"She does love to explore." Ally smiled.

"Ally, I know why you're really here." Tanya frowned as she stepped closer to her. "You don't have to make up stories."

"Good. Then I'm glad you're alone." Ally met her eyes as her heart continued to pound.

"You are?" Tanya crossed her arms. "Why is that?"

"I know none of this can be easy. I can see how close you and Becca are. You're probably very protective of her, right? Being her older cousin and all." Ally leaned her shoulder against the back of the house.

"I can be, I guess. We are very close, we have always been." Tanya shrugged as she studied her. "What's your point?"

"My point is, as heartbreaking as it must have been for Becca to find out that Vinnie had lied to her it must have been upsetting to you, too, right? You and Gus had embraced Vinnie, you had welcomed him into your family, only to have him turn out to be a liar. That would have upset me for sure." Ally pursed her lips at the thought.

"Of course it was upsetting." Tanya shrugged. "But Becca's a big girl. I knew she could handle her own problems. I didn't see a reason to get into the middle of it."

"No?" Ally raised an eyebrow. "Because yesterday when I asked Becca if a large man with a mustache asked her about Vinnie, you immediately left the room. I have to wonder why that was. You seemed eager to get away from the question. So now, I'd like to know. Have you seen him?"

"What does it matter?" Tanya met her eyes. "What difference does it make if I saw him?"

"It makes a big difference, especially if there's a reason why you're not admitting to it." Ally crossed the distance between them. "I've spoken to him, Tanya. I was alone with him, and I'll be honest, he scared me a bit. He has a very intense presence, not to mention his size. If he threatened you, I can understand why you would be afraid. But the police can protect you."

"The police who haven't managed to solve Vinnie's murder yet?" Tanya cleared her throat. "Thanks, but no thanks."

"So, you did see him?" Ally searched her eyes. "Are you scared of him?"

"I'm not scared of him." Tanya sighed, then shook her head.

"It's time you told the truth, Tanya." Ally held her

gaze. "A man has been killed, a man who was going to be part of your family. Don't you think your cousin deserves some answers?"

"Don't talk to me about what my cousin deserves!" Tanya glared at her. "She deserves better than that swindler could have ever given her! I trusted him!" She wiped her hand across her eyes as she looked away from her. "When Vinnie started dating her, I spoke to him. I told him I would do anything I could to protect my cousin, and that he'd better not hurt her. She's already been through so much. When Cliff broke things off with her, I thought she'd never recover, she was so heartbroken. I swore I would never let someone hurt her that way again." She dropped her hand to her side and gasped. "But I didn't see it! Vinnie lied to me, he told me that he would take good care of her, that he would never hurt her. He lied to me the entire time, and I didn't see it! I couldn't protect her!"

"What do you mean?" Ally tried to keep up with her words as they spilled out. "Because his business wasn't legitimate?"

"His business?" Tanya laughed. "You have no idea what his business was!" She shook her head. "Yes, I saw Joe. He was outside the hotel, arguing with the woman from the flower shop. I thought no man should be talking to a woman that way, so I went over there and interrupted them. She took off, and that's when Joe told me why he was there."

"What did he say exactly?" Ally held her breath.

"He said he was hired to hunt down Vinnie." Tanya frowned. "He said that Vinnie was using false identification. Vinnie was a con artist."

"Wait, are you saying that Vinnie wasn't who he said he was?" Ally's heartbeat quickened as she realized that Tanya knew the truth about Vinnie, or at least what Joe said was the truth. That certainly gave her motive. "Are you sure about that?"

"What can I be sure of at this point?" Tanya rolled her eyes. "I already knew that Vinnie had been lying about his business. Cliff told Gus about that, and he told me about it. But this was different. Joe told me that Vinnie makes a living doing this. He cons women into marrying him. He pretends to be someone else, uses a fake identity, and marries the women, only to disappear with everything he can steal from his bride and her family." She crossed her arms.

"And you believed him? Did he have any proof of this?" Ally raised an eyebrow. "Maybe Joe made it all up."

"Maybe he did. He claimed he knew of other people that Vinnie had done this to. I didn't want to hear anymore from him. I knew I had to stop the wedding, no matter what. Vinnie wasn't who he said he was, and I couldn't let my cousin marry him." Tanya took a step back and closed her eyes. "If only I had done a better job of protecting her from the beginning, maybe none of this would have happened. Instead, I let myself believe that Vinnie was the person he claimed to be, and he almost ruined her life."

"That must have made you so angry." Ally's eyes widened as she realized that Tanya had plenty of motive to kill Vinnie, and her only alibi was that she was with her uncle and cousin. She already knew that Becca had lied about being with Tanya all morning as she had actually met up with Vinnie, she guessed that Gus could easily be lying, too.

"Don't start with that." Tanya's voice sharpened as she settled her gaze on her. "I didn't kill him. I love my cousin, but I could never do that!"

"You love her so much that you would keep all of this from her?" Ally shook her head. "Don't you think she had a right to know?"

"Yes, I did think that. Which is why I told her." Tanya frowned and crossed her arms again. "I'm still not sure if it was the right thing to do. But like you said, she had a right to know."

"She knew that Vinnie was a con artist? When did you tell her?"

"When she came back from the coffee shop. She had confronted him about the business, but she thought they could still work things out. That's when I broke down and told her everything. I just couldn't have her believing this man was worth marrying." Tanya shook her head. "She was furious, said I had been lying to her as much as he had. But I hadn't been." She squeezed her hands into fists. "I just didn't want to hurt her."

"Of course you didn't." Alarm bells rang in Ally's mind as she took a step back from Tanya. Becca knew everything? She knew her future husband intended to steal every dime he could from her and then abandon her? With her heart shattered, she had plenty of motive to kill Vinnie. "I need to talk to Becca, Tanya."

"She's not here." Tanya shook her head. "She left early this morning. I don't know where she went. I've been trying to track her down. Hopefully, she'll be back soon." She sighed as she looked into Ally's eyes. "I only want to help her."

"I know you do, Tanya. I want to help her, too."

Ally's chest tightened as she spoke those words. Maybe Vinnie had been a criminal, but that didn't mean that he deserved to die. If Becca had killed him, even in a fit of rage, she would have to face the consequences. "Let me know if you hear from her."

CHAPTER 16

*lly reached the cottage just as her grandmother stepped out the door with Arnold and Peaches on leashes by her side.

"Ally, I've been calling you!" Charlotte frowned. "You said you wouldn't be too long."

"I'm sorry, Mee-Maw. I had my phone on silent. I was driving." Ally sighed. "And trying to figure things out."

"Let's go for a walk?" Charlotte headed down the driveway.

"Sure." Ally took Peaches' leash and followed after her as she filled her in on what Tanya had confessed. "At this point, I don't see how it could be anyone other than Becca. She had the most motive.

She could have lured him, or even driven him, to the barn. She's a strong woman and Vinnie was a small man. In a fit of rage I could see her being able to strangle Vinnie."

"It does add up." Charlotte pulled Arnold back from a tree he started sniffing. "I'm sure Luke will be able to arrest her with this information."

"But I don't have any proof." Ally waved to her neighbor with her free hand. "But she is definitely getting higher on my suspect list. It turns out Cliff is the one who broke up with Becca. To go through that, and then face the truth about Vinnie, I wouldn't be surprised if she snapped." She nodded. "But I still don't want to believe that she did it."

"We need to explore all avenues. If she did this, she has to be held accountable for her actions." Charlotte glanced over at her. "Whether or not we like Vinnie, it's still his murder that we're trying to solve. And we need to explore all avenues, including Becca."

"You're right." Ally nodded and started back toward the cottage. "We are going to have to find Becca, and hope that she will talk to us."

"I think she's more likely to talk to us than the police." Charlotte opened the cottage door.

Ally checked Arnold and Peaches' water bowls and said goodbye to them, then stepped outside. "I still hope deep down that Becca didn't do this."

"I understand." Charlotte followed her to the car. "But the amount of motive she had after what Tanya told her, it's hard to dismiss that, especially since she's been hiding her knowledge of it this whole time."

"Maybe." Ally started the car, then glanced over at her grandmother. "Or maybe it didn't leave her as heartbroken as we think. She certainly put on a good show when she discovered Vinnie was dead. She acted as if she was shocked, that she had no idea that he had been killed. But she also behaved as if she had lost the love of her life. Knowing now, that she was aware of his con, all of that must have been a lie, right? She wouldn't have been so heartbroken over the loss of a man who conned and scammed her, would she?"

"I would guess not. But the heart can be quite fickle, Ally. Just because he betrayed her, that doesn't necessarily mean that she didn't still love him."

"Unless she never loved him in the first place." Ally turned down the street in the direction of Vinnie's house. "Hopefully, she'll be back at the house and Tanya hasn't warned her that she told me the truth. But she might have. I think at this point, Tanya just wants to help her in any way that she can."

"Or frame her." Charlotte raised an eyebrow. "We haven't ruled her out as a suspect either."

"That's true." Ally sighed. "She could be trying to convince me that she's on my side, to make herself look innocent. But could she really do that to her cousin?"

"If she's afraid she will go to prison, maybe." Charlotte shrugged.

"I wish I could just get inside Becca's head and have an idea of what she really felt for Vinnie. Did she really want to marry him as much as she made it seem? Did she just agree to it because of how wealthy he appeared?"

"You think she might not have loved Vinnie at all?" Charlotte raised an eyebrow. "What makes you think that?"

"I just think it's interesting that Cliff was there right away, when Vinnie died. He's also the one who looked deep enough into Vinnie's business to figure out that he was up to no good. He claims their relationship ended, but it seems to me that it might not have been completely over."

"Interesting." Charlotte nodded. "It's possible that

they still have something between them. But if so, why would Becca have chosen to marry Vinnie?"

"If Cliff is the one that broke up with her, and broke her heart in the process, maybe she wanted him back. Maybe she thought accepting a marriage proposal from someone else would light a fire under Cliff. She could have been conning Vinnie. Maybe she had her hopes pinned on Cliff intervening and declaring his love."

"Or maybe, she just wanted his money." Charlotte sighed as she looked out through the windshield.

"Maybe. It's a terrible thought, though." Ally frowned. "I hope she didn't do this. I couldn't imagine killing anyone, let alone the person I planned to marry."

"I'm sure you can't. But what if you chose someone else, and lost your chance with Luke, and it turned out that the person you chose was a con artist?" Charlotte frowned. "That might be enough to make you snap and do something that you never thought you would."

"Not me, no." Ally tightened her grip on the steering wheel. "But maybe Becca." She tipped her head toward the driveway they pulled up to. "Her car is here now. I wonder if she will talk to us."

"Only one way to find out." Charlotte stepped out of the car.

Ally followed her to the front door.

The moment that Becca opened it, Ally noticed puffiness around her eyes.

"Becca, are you okay?"

"No." Becca stared at them both. "Of course, I'm not okay."

"I'm sorry, I'm sure you're not." Ally frowned as she looked into her reddened eyes. "Could we come in for a minute? We'd like to talk to you about something."

"Are you here to accuse me of murdering my Vinnie?" Becca sniffled. "Because if you are, it's too late. The police have already been here to do that."

"What?" Ally's eyes widened. "They were here?"

"Just left. Apparently, they have some new information and wanted me to account for every minute of my time the morning that Vinnie was killed." Becca clutched the tissues in her hand tighter. "Do you have any idea how painful it is to think about what I was doing as someone murdered the love of my life?"

"Becca, we know the truth about Vinnie being a conman, and we know that you know it, too."

Charlotte looked at her. "You may have convinced the police that you don't know anything, but we both know that you do, and that you knew before Vinnie was killed."

"What are you saying?" Becca glared at Charlotte. "How do you know all of this?"

"I told them." Tanya stepped out from the kitchen, behind her cousin. "I told them everything, Becca. I'm sorry. I would do anything to protect you, but Vinnie is dead!"

"Tanya!" Becca gasped as she took a step back into the house. "How could you?" Her eyes widened. "Tanya, do you think I killed him? You can't possibly think that!"

"I don't know what to think." Tanya winced as she stepped between her and Ally and Charlotte. "Becca, I only know that I wanted to kill him, and it must have been so much more painful for you. Maybe if you come forward, and tell the truth now, you'll be able to make some kind of deal. I just think you need to be honest about everything. It's the only way to make sure you'll be okay."

"Wow." Becca squeezed her eyes shut, then shook her head. "I didn't think this could get any worse, but it just did." She turned to face her cousin. "Why do you think the police didn't arrest me?"

"I don't know." Tanya frowned as she took her hand. "I'm just glad that they didn't."

"They didn't arrest me, because I showed them proof that it wasn't me. That I loved Vinnie." Becca pulled her phone out of her pocket. "After you told me the whole truth, I went back to Vinnie and confronted him. He confessed everything. But he insisted that he wanted to leave that life behind, that all he wanted was to marry me, and start a new life." She sighed as she pressed a button on her phone. "Just listen."

What Ally assumed must be Vinnie's voice played through the speaker on the phone.

"Please, give me a chance to prove myself to you, Becca. You'll see, I only want to be with you. I know it will take a lot for you to forgive me, but I can be patient. I never expected to fall in love, but now I have, and I don't want to live without you."

Becca's voice played through the speaker next.

"You're a liar, and a con artist, and you intended to steal everything from me. How do you expect me to believe you?"

Becca paused the recording. "I recorded our conversation as a way to prove to the police what he was up to. But instead, it ended up recording me promising to help him." She pressed play again.

"I see it in your eyes, Becca. You can hate me, you can be furious with me, but you can't deny it, can you? You still love me as much as I love you."

"I do." Becca's voice on the recording cracked, followed by an audible gasp. "I must be the stupidest person on this earth, but I do still love you."

"Then you must help me. If we move quickly, we can escape all of this. But we have to do it fast."

Becca pressed pause on the recording again, then looked into Ally's eyes. "So, there's the truth. I fell for him. I have no idea if he really loved me, or if he planned to steal from me in the end, but on the morning that he was killed, I still wanted to be with him. I didn't murder the man I loved, even if he had told me that he had scammed me, that I was nothing to him, I still couldn't have murdered him. Don't you know that yourself, Ally? Is there anything that Luke could do that would make you want to take his life?"

"No." Ally shook her head. "But I've also never been faced with what you were faced with."

"When he realized that someone was in town, that knew about his past, he told me that his only connection to his last scam, was the car he was driving. He had to get rid of it." Becca took a deep breath. "I told him I would take care of it. He loved me, and he wanted to marry me, and we wanted to start a new life together. I guess I thought getting rid of his only connection to his past would help me feel better, too. So, I dropped him off at the barn, I knew my father would drive me there for our appointment later in the day and we could meet up. It seemed like a safe place for him to hide out with Joe roaming around town."

"That makes sense." Ally nodded.

"I drove the car to the next town and dumped it, then I took a taxi back to his house. I showed the police the charge for the taxi, and the length of the ride I took. Which made them see that I wasn't anywhere near Vinnie in his last moments."

"So, you have a solid alibi?" Ally tried to meet her eyes.

"Yes." Becca sighed. "I can't expect you to understand. I'm sure you're thinking, I was insane to still think he loved me. Maybe I was." She shrugged as a few tears slipped down her cheeks. "Maybe he really was conning me. But the way he looked at me, the way he spoke to me." She clutched her hands together and pressed them against her chest. "No one has ever made me feel that way. Not even Cliff. It was like he wanted to change his entire life for me.

He'd made his living from faking romance, but ours turned out to be real. After I learned he died, I just couldn't let anyone find out the truth about him. It was too upsetting. It was too embarrassing."

Ally bit into her bottom lip. She did feel the urge to judge Becca. Of course, a conman didn't just flip a switch and become a loving husband. But she tried to imagine how she'd feel if it turned out Luke had lied to her about something so important. She would be devastated, but she knew she might still long for him.

"After you left him at the barn, you never spoke to him again?" Ally's eyes narrowed. "Are you telling the truth this time?"

"Yes, I'm telling the truth. I didn't speak to him at all. You can check my phone. No calls came in or went out after I called him the first time that morning." Becca held out her phone to her. "Go on, look for yourself, Ally. I can't expect you to believe me, I don't really believe myself. But it's what happened. When I dropped him off at the barn, he was alive, and in love, and we had a plan to get out of all of this, together. When I returned, he was already gone." A sob escaped her lips as she accepted her phone back from Ally. "I still can't believe he's really gone."

Ally's heart sank as she watched the woman tremble with grief. Maybe it was all an act, but if it was, she deserved an award for it.

"I'm sorry, Becca." Ally looked into her eyes. "No matter what the truth was, you lost someone you loved dearly. You did everything you could to protect him."

"Yes, I did." Becca wiped at her eyes. "I can't talk about this anymore. I'm sorry, I just can't. I hope you figure out who did this, but there's nothing else I have to offer."

"We understand." Charlotte nodded to her, then looked over at Tanya. "For what it's worth, I would have loved to have a cousin who was so determined to help and protect me." She glanced back at Becca. "She only wanted the best for you."

"I know." Becca nodded. "She always has."

As Becca pushed the door shut, Ally looked over at her grandmother.

"Well, I think we can cross our main suspect off the list." Ally sighed. "Which doesn't leave us with much to go on."

"It may not seem like it, but it is getting us closer to the truth. We know how Vinnie ended up at the barn without his car. We have an idea of who he saw and spoke to that morning. Our window of opportunity is much smaller now as well. We're going in the right direction." Charlotte hooked her arm through Ally's as they walked toward the car.

CHAPTER 17

*V*innie's voice from the recording echoed through Ally's mind.

"We know that one person knows exactly what happened to Vinnie. Or at least, he is the most likely to." Ally looked at her grandmother. "We need to find Joe. He's been involved in all of this from the start. He was sent here to find Vinnie, and he's most likely the one who killed him. We know that he wanted to buy a gas can, which means he likely planned to burn down the barn with Vinnie in it."

"Although, I have to say, that's odd. Don't you think?" Charlotte frowned. "First of all, why wouldn't your average person know where to buy a gas can? Secondly, why would a murderer leave that kind of trail behind by asking about it? And why can't Luke find any proof that he bought it?"

"I don't know. Maybe Joe isn't as smart as we think. But no matter what, we need to find him and figure out what he knows once and for all." Ally fished her phone out of her purse. "And I know just how to track him down." She dialed Mrs. Bing's phone number.

As they settled into the car, Ally received an earful about Joe's most recent sightings.

"According to Mrs. Bing he's been at the diner, and also the library. But the last place she saw him headed was the florist in Blue River."

"Remember what you told me Tanya said about interrupting Joe and Gloria as they argued at the hotel?" Charlotte frowned. "Why would Gloria be arguing with him? She acted so frightened of him when she told us about seeing him in the florist. But she didn't say a word about arguing with him at the hotel."

"You're right." Ally drove toward the florist. "Why wouldn't she mention that to us or to Luke?"

"She must be hiding it for a reason." Charlotte shook her head. "But I can't imagine why. Maybe she decided to confront Joe, before he had the chance to ruin the wedding between Vinnie and

Becca. Maybe she just didn't want to lose the business?"

"I'm not so sure about that." Ally frowned as she considered the possibility. "She mentioned that she had a terrible experience with her own wedding. I don't think she takes these ceremonies lightly. If anything, maybe she would have confronted him to find out the truth about Vinnie." She frowned as she parked outside of the florist.

They got out of the car and walked toward the large front window of the shop.

"Ally, he's in there." Charlotte pointed toward the window. "And he doesn't look happy!"

Through the window, Ally saw Joe swing his hands through the air as he shouted at Gloria.

"Oh no! We'd better get in there!" Ally charged toward the door and swung it open just as Joe shouted.

"I'm not leaving until you tell me the truth!"

"What's going on here?" Charlotte stepped in behind Ally, her tone stern.

"None of your business!" Joe shot her a sharp look before he turned back to Gloria. "This is between the two of us."

"Now, it's between the four of us." Ally surveyed the large man's body language as he shot a quick look in her direction. He turned his attention right back to Gloria.

"You are the reason I'm in this mess!" Joe glared at her as he lunged toward the front counter. "Why did you tell the police that I was trying to buy a gas can?"

"Get out of my shop!" Gloria's voice raised higher than Joe's as she rounded the counter. "You have no right to be here! Get out of my shop before I call the police!"

"Oh yes, you call them! Please do, right now." Joe smacked his hand into one of the nearby shelves and sent a few vases flying to the floor.

As the glass shattered, Gloria shrieked.

"That's it!" Charlotte charged forward, despite Ally's attempt to grab her arm. "You can't come in here and start destroying things, I don't care who you are!" Charlotte stepped between him and Gloria.

"Mee-Maw!" Ally gasped as she hurried to her side. "What are you doing? He's a murderer!"

"I'm no murderer!" Joe scowled at them. "But that's what she would like you to believe! Isn't it, Gloria?" He shook his head as he took a few steps back. "I thought I was going to help you, Gloria. I thought that I would make things right for you. But instead you've turned all of this around on me. I'm not going to let it go! Do you hear me? I'm not going to prison for you!"

"You've lost your mind!" Gloria threw her hands up in the air. "You've absolutely lost your mind! I have no idea who you are or why you are in my shop, but you need to leave right now!"

"I'm going." A low chuckle escaped his lips. "But I'll be back, I promise you that."

"Is that a threat?" Ally stepped between him and the door. "I'm sure that the police would like to know about you threatening an innocent woman."

"Innocent?" Joe raised an eyebrow. "She sure does look it, doesn't she?" He glared at her, then pushed past her toward the door.

"If you have something to say, Joe, we're here, we're listening." Charlotte met him at the door. "Tell us exactly what you think happened to Vinnie?"

"Vinnie's dead." Joe looked into Charlotte's eyes as his voice darkened. "I think you should be more concerned with the people who are still alive, and what might happen to them." He glanced over his shoulder at Gloria. "A woman scorned will do anything to get revenge, won't she, Gloria?"

"What does that mean?" Ally's heartbeat quickened as she reached for Joe's arm.

CINDY BELL

He stepped through the door, and out of her reach, before she could catch him.

"Oh no, he's not getting away that easily." Charlotte reached for the door knob to follow after him. Gloria's hand closed around it before she could get to it.

"I can't let you do that, Charlotte." Gloria twisted the lock on the door, then turned to face Charlotte and Ally.

CHAPTER 18

*A*lly stared at Gloria. "What are you doing, Gloria?"

"Let us out, we have to stop him!" Charlotte reached for the lock.

"He could hurt someone else!" Ally tried to push past Gloria.

"Don't." Gloria flattened her back against the door and blocked it. "You shouldn't go after him. He's a dangerous man!"

"Gloria, we have to!" Ally tried to nudge her aside from the door.

"No!" Gloria glared at them both. "You're not leaving here! Do you understand me?"

"Not at all!" Charlotte gasped as she glared back

at her. "You can't keep us here! Don't you want him to be caught?"

"Mee-Maw." Ally grabbed her hand and tugged her back away from Gloria. Her heart lurched into a rhythm she'd never experienced before in the same moment that her throat tightened.

"Ally, what are you doing?" Charlotte frowned.

"She's not trying to protect us." Ally looked around for another exit from the small building. If there was a back door, it was hidden behind shelving.

"What?" Charlotte's eyes widened. "Gloria! This isn't true, is it?"

Ally lunged toward the large front window.

"Don't!" Gloria grabbed her around the waist and pulled her away from it. "Stop!" Her voice shifted into a shriek. "Everything is getting out of control! It has to stop!" She pulled a string, and blinds cascaded down across the front window. "I just need to think for a moment!"

"What is there to think about?" Charlotte scowled. "You must let us out this second!"

"She's not going to do that, Mee-Maw." Ally crossed her arms as she stared at Gloria. "Because she's the one that murdered Vinnie."

"I'm not a murderer!" Gloria slumped over and slapped her hands hard against her own thighs as she sucked down a sharp breath. "Don't call me that! He was an evil man, he deserved to be punished for his terrible acts!"

"He conned you, didn't he, Gloria?" Charlotte stepped closer to Gloria as she stood up straighter. "He tricked you into marrying him, and then he broke your heart, didn't he?"

"Yes, of course he did! Just like he's done before and after, numerous times! He ruined so many lives!" The fury that seeped off of Gloria's words seemed to heat up the air around her as she neared Ally. "He had no right to shatter my heart into a million pieces! I'd built a life for myself! I'd earned my way into college, then paid for the tuition when my family couldn't! I landed a wonderful job and worked hard for the income I received. I was always careful with my money, making sure that I saved it instead of spending it on even the most enticing things."

"That sounds wonderful." Charlotte tried to calm her down. "You did an amazing job."

"It was wonderful. I was so proud of myself." Grief crept into Gloria's voice as she shook her head.

"Not because of my money and success, though that was great. I was proud because I was so happy. Then that monster entered my life." She squeezed her hands into fists. "My family never liked him. They encouraged me to see other people, and of course, I got so angry at them for saying that. If only I had listened to them. I didn't talk to them for the longest two weeks of my life. But I loved him and I chose him over them, really. Eventually they learned to like him. I could tell they were doing their best to be supportive." She wiped at her cheeks as a few tears slid down them. "When he proposed, I was so excited. I accepted of course. He was welcomed into my family."

"Then everything went wrong?" Ally took a step toward her.

"Yes." Gloria clenched her hands into fists. "We got married and less than two weeks later he just disappeared. Took everything he could with him. All my things, all my hard earned money. All the money I had been saving to start a business. Money my parents had given us when we got married. Money they scraped together for me. Do you know how much I had to borrow to start this florist. He ruined everything. I found out he had been using someone else's identity and he was nowhere to be found."

"It must have been so devastating when the truth came out." Ally reached for her hand. "The police will understand that you weren't in your right mind, Gloria. All you have to do is tell the truth."

"Oh no, that won't work." Gloria patted Ally's hand as she smiled. "No, you see, I was in my right mind. I thought if I moved here I would be able to get over it, but of course I couldn't, what he did to me was always on my mind. When Vinnie and Becca came to pick out their flowers, I couldn't believe my eyes. Vinnie stayed outside, by the car, but I could see him clearly enough. I recognized him straight away of course." She took a deep breath. "All I wanted was for him to pay back everything he took from me, and to admit what he'd done. I'd been blaming myself for his treachery. I just wanted him to apologize to me and help me finally get over what he had done to me, and prove that it wasn't my fault."

"So, you went to speak to him?" Ally peered into her eyes.

"Yes, I had to talk to him. He had disappeared with no explanation. I had no idea what to think. Yes, I wanted him to apologize to me and pay me back, pay for what he had done, I needed my questions answered." Gloria leaned back against the door and closed her eyes for just an instant before she continued. "We almost ran into each other at the barn, when he argued with Blake and I saw him push him. Vinnie was such a terrible man, such a bully. I went to the hotel where Becca's family was staying. That's where I ran into Joe. He recognized me and told me he wanted to talk to me."

"What a coincidence." Ally's eyes widened.

"It was. Maybe it was fate. He was hired by one of Vinnie's other victim brides to find Vinnie. We went into Joe's room and he showed me files he had of some of the women that Vinnie, or whatever his real name was, did this to. He had pictures of my wedding, he recognized me from them. When he told me how many women Vinnie had done this to, when he showed me all of the pictures, it broke me." Gloria looked between the two of them as fresh tears began to flow. "To think that all of those women suffered the same fate as me, and he was about to do it again. Joe wanted me to tell him where Vinnie was, where he lived. But I couldn't." She shook her head. "I didn't want to put Becca at risk, and I also didn't want him to get Vinnie arrested before I had the chance to confront him. So, I told him I didn't know."

"You made the entire thing up, about Joe scaring

you, about him looking for a gas can?" Ally frowned as she recalled just how quickly she was to believe that Joe could be the killer. "You were trying to pin the murder on him?"

"I just needed a little more time." A sob broke through Gloria's words. "I didn't mean to kill Vinnie. I brought the rope there, just to restrain him, to keep him from getting away before I could get the truth from him. But when I got to the barn, he didn't apologize. He laughed in my face. He told me I'd never be able to prove anything, and that he and Becca would be gone before the police ever caught up with him. It was then that I realized he wasn't planning to con Becca. He was planning to actually be with her."

"That must have been a shock." Ally's eyes widened.

"It was more than a shock. It made me furious. My life had been shattered by him, so many other women suffered the same fate, and he was going to get the 'happily ever after' he stole from them, that he stole from me." Gloria trembled as her voice sharpened. "No! I couldn't let that happen! I was just so angry. I didn't even think about it. Next thing I knew the rope was around his neck."

"Oh Gloria." Charlotte sighed as she stared at the

189

trembling woman. "You had so many other options. You had proof that could have convicted him. You had Joe who had even more proof."

"And how long would he have gone to jail for?" Gloria glared at her. "A few years at best? And then he would just get out and do it again. Prison wasn't enough for him. He deserved a real punishment." She looked down at her hands and drew in a deep breath. "I didn't think I was ever capable of such a thing, but then, it was over, and he was on the ground."

"So, you set fire to the barn as well?" Ally looked at her.

"Yes, I knew I had to cover up what I did. Not that it helped any. I remembered seeing a gas can quite close to the barn. I grabbed it. I had matches in my purse. I didn't go there intending to kill him, or to set the barn on fire. I just did what I had to do." Gloria's voice became strong.

"But how did you even know he was there?" Ally crossed her arms. "He was hiding out, according to Becca."

"Because I called him, and he answered." Gloria smiled, then rolled her eyes. "For being a con artist he wasn't that bright. He must have thought it was someone else. But once he answered, I knew where he was. I could hear those birds that he convinced Blake to get. After I set the barn on fire, I managed to get back to the shop just in time to meet the two of you. I thought the barn would be completely destroyed and so would any evidence before anyone could do anything. I guess I didn't use enough gas." She wiped her hand across her face. "I didn't plan to kill him. I was just going to talk to him. But he was so smug, and so—" Her voice cracked as she struggled to take a breath. "So in love!"

Ally's heart dropped as those words echoed through her mind. Becca had been right to believe that Vinnie loved her. After all of his terrible crimes, he'd come across a woman that he'd fallen in love with.

"We can help you." Ally shivered as she stared at Gloria. "You know Luke, you know that he will do what he can to help you. All you have to do is explain what happened to him. You weren't in your right mind, you made a mistake, we both know that. Don't we, Mee-Maw?"

Ally glanced over at her.

"Yes, of course we do." Charlotte's hand curled around a large vase on a shelf beside her. She shifted her body in an attempt to block her actions.

"No." Gloria shook her head. "It's too late for

that. I covered up my crime. I tried to frame Joe for it. No jury is going to have sympathy for me." She took a deep breath. "The important thing is that he can never hurt anyone else the way he hurt me, and all of those other women. If it means that I have to spend the rest of my life on the run, so be it."

"On the run?" Ally frowned. "What makes you think you can get away with that? Once the truth gets out—"

"The truth isn't going to get out." Gloria glared at them both.

"Where do you think Joe is right now?" Ally stepped in front of Charlotte to block the vase she held from view. "He figured it out, I'm sure he's talking to the police right now."

"No, he's not." Gloria shook her head. "Joe was trying to avoid the police. I imagine he has his own past to run from. I'm sure that he's already headed to the next state, and then the border. Because with no one that can prove otherwise, he's still the best suspect out there." She sighed as she looked between the two of them. "Which brings me to the problem of the two of you." She walked around behind the counter and picked up a gas can. "I kept this. I thought I'd just get rid of it at some point. But it turns out, it's going to come in handy. I think there's just enough gasoline left to start a good fire going."

"Don't Gloria!" Ally gasped as she heard the splash of liquid against the wooden counter.

"I'm sorry, I know this isn't pleasant or kind." Gloria winced. "But I've learned, I have to do what I have to do to take care of me." As she splashed more gasoline around, Charlotte charged forward with the vase in her hand.

Gloria spun around to face her just as Charlotte swung the vase through the air.

Gloria jumped to the side, as Charlotte slid through the puddle of gasoline on the floor.

Ally managed to catch her before she could hit the floor.

"Well, look at that." Gloria smiled as the vase shattered against the tile floor. "It's not that hard to do what you need to protect yourself is it, Charlotte?" She watched the pair as Ally helped her grandmother find her balance.

"You can't justify this, Gloria!" Charlotte glared at her. "You can't murder us, and think that you're still innocent!"

"I haven't been innocent since the moment I saw Vinnie and Becca together. I haven't been innocent since I made the decision to get justice for what

Vinnie did to me. Now, all that matters is that I escape." Gloria pulled a pack of matches from her purse. "You're going to have to forgive me, I can't stick around to keep you company." She pulled out a match from the box.

CHAPTER 19

*I*n the same moment that Gloria went to strike the match, glass shattered behind her. Ally dove forward and knocked the match out of her hand before it ignited.

Hands and feet thrust through the broken front window of the shop.

"I'm tangled!" Mrs. Bing's voice shrieked. Ally immediately recognized it.

"Just tug it down!" Mrs. White huffed as a pair of hands yanked at the blinds.

"Ally!" Mrs. Cale poked her head around one side of the blinds. "Ally and Charlotte, are you in there?"

Gloria ran for the shelves at the back of the shop. She tried to shove them out of the way of the back door.

"No, you don't!" Charlotte grabbed her around the waist and tugged her down to the floor. "You're not getting away with this! Vinnie might have done some terrible things, but you are a murderer!"

Gloria struggled to get back to her feet as Ally tried to help her grandmother keep her down on the floor.

"Allow me." Mrs. Bing huffed as she plopped down onto Gloria's back. She crossed her arms as she looked at Ally and Charlotte. "Aren't you two lucky to have friends like us?"

"We certainly are." Ally glanced at the match on the floor. She shivered as she thought of what could have happened. "We certainly are lucky to have all of you." Tears glazed her eyes as Mrs. Cale and Mrs. White walked over to them. "How did you know to come to our rescue?"

"As soon as you called and wanted to know where Joe was seen, I guessed that you were up to something." Mrs. Bing clucked her tongue. "Of course, I wasn't sure just what."

"I thought you were planning to set a trap for him." Mrs. Cale smirked.

"I thought you were going to end up in a big mess, like you did." Mrs. White rolled her eyes as she placed her hands on her hips. "To think of what might have happened if we hadn't shown up when we did." She sighed. "What were you waiting for, the police to show up?"

As the shrill sound of a siren blared outside the shop, Ally felt relief wash over her.

"There's Luke, now."

"It's about time!" Mrs. White pursed her lips. "He'd better not be this late on your wedding day!"

"Enough!" Mrs. Bing snapped her fingers. "You know as well as I do that he won't be one second late."

Ally stared down at the woman still pinned beneath Mrs. Bing. As much as she didn't want to feel it, sympathy bubbled up within her. She was a murderer, yes, but she was also a heartbroken bride.

"Was it worth it, Gloria?"

"Absolutely, I did what I had to do." Gloria attempted to wriggle out from under Mrs. Bing.

"I'm not going anywhere." Mrs. Bing crossed her arms.

Charlotte unlocked the door as Luke pounded on it.

"Charlotte?" He frowned, then looked past her at Ally. "I heard reports of three women breaking through the front window?" His eyes flicked across Mrs. White, and Mrs. Cale, then settled on Mrs.

Bing. "What are you doing to Gloria?" His eyes widened.

"It's a citizen's arrest!" Mrs. Bing shrugged. "We don't all lug handcuffs around you know."

"Gloria is the one who killed Vinnie." Ally wrapped her arm around her grandmother's waist. "Then she planned to trap us in here, and set the florist on fire."

"What?" Fury rippled across Luke's face, a moment before a calm authority possessed it once again. "Thank you, Mrs. Bing, I'll take it from here."

As Mrs. Bing got to her feet, Luke closed handcuffs around Gloria's wrists.

Ally watched him pull her to her feet, then turn her toward the door. As he read her her rights, she listened to his stern, even voice, and felt the familiar peace that his presence brought her. The terror of moments before, seemed a lifetime away.

"Are you okay, Ally?" Charlotte leaned her head against the side of Ally's.

"I am now." Ally met her eyes. "Thanks to you, and our friends, and Luke."

Patrol cars arrived in front of the shop. Ally took a deep breath of the gasoline-scented air, then shook her head.

"Let's go outside, Mee-Maw. I don't want to be

here a moment longer." She grabbed her grandmother's hand and they walked toward the door.

Outside the shop, many residents had gathered, drawn by the flashing lights.

Luke placed Gloria in the backseat of his car, then strode over to Ally.

"Are you hurt?" He took both of her hands.

"Not at all." Ally smiled, then glanced at her grandmother. "We're both okay, aren't we, Mee-Maw?"

"Not a scratch." Charlotte nodded, then winked at Ally. "Thanks to my quick-footed granddaughter."

"You should have seen the way she wielded a vase!" Ally felt a laugh bubble up in her throat. It seemed wrong to laugh, as the lights splashed across broken glass on the sidewalk, and her neighbors gossiped about what might have happened. But in that moment she had to admit she was happy. Happy that the murderer had been found, happy that she and her grandmother had made it out safely, and happy that now she could feel the rush of excitement for her impending wedding once more.

"I'd better get her to the station. We solved Vinnie's murder, and I found out that Vinnie's supposed ex-business partner that disappeared, presumed murdered, was actually one of Vinnie's aliases. Vinnie fabricated his murder so he could con one of his brides out of her money." Luke nodded. "This will lead to a lot of women getting closure for what he did to them."

"Go make sure you have a solid case." Ally met his eyes.

Luke nodded as he turned away.

As Ally watched him walk away, she realized that she didn't want to wait a moment longer to marry him. But she would have to.

"Let's go home, Ally." Charlotte took her arm and gave it a light squeeze.

Ally knew she meant the cottage. Even though Charlotte lived at Freely Lakes now, the cottage would always be their home.

Still in a daze, she hugged Mrs. Bing, then Mrs. White, and finally Mrs. Cale.

"I will never give you three a hard time about gossiping or being nosy again."

"That's a lie!" Mrs. White laughed. Then she patted Ally's cheek. "We're just glad you're okay, darling. Never forget, you have a whole town looking out for you."

"I couldn't be luckier." Ally smiled, then followed her grandmother to the car.

On the short drive to the cottage, Ally ran through Gloria's confession in her mind.

"I still can't quite believe it, Mee-Maw. Gloria seemed like such a normal person, and yet she was a murderer." Ally stepped out of the car.

"What Gloria did was terrible." Charlotte draped her arm across Ally's shoulders. "A broken heart is a powerful thing."

"It is." Ally unlocked the door and smiled. "I think I need a good sleep. At least the wedding is something to look forward to."

"Yes, yes it is." Charlotte smiled back as Peaches and Arnold ran to the door to greet them.

Ally and Charlotte crouched down.

"Hi babies." Ally ran her hand over their backs.

"It's nice being home." Charlotte kissed Arnold on the head.

"The best." Ally smiled.

CHAPTER 20

"Wake up!" Charlotte rubbed Ally's shoulder. "Let's go, time to get up."

"What? Why?" Ally peered at her grandmother. "The shop is closed today, I can sleep as late as I want." She sighed as she looked toward the window. "It's barely daylight."

"No time to waste." Charlotte shooed her out of bed. "Have a shower. Get some clothes on, you've got a special assignment."

"Huh?" Ally stumbled around as she struggled to fully awaken.

Peaches rubbed against her legs as Arnold sniffed her hand. She bent down to pat them.

"Mee-Maw, it's so early." Ally walked into the kitchen with the pets close behind.

"Come on, let's go. I'll take care of Arnold and Peaches." Charlotte guided her to a fresh cup of coffee on the counter. "Take that to go."

"Where?" Frustration mounted within Ally as she tried to understand her grandmother's rambling. "Mee-Maw!"

"Please Ally, I need you to take care of this for me. I know it's a lot to ask when you've been through so much, but if you don't do it, no one will. Just go with Luke please. He knows the whole plan."

"I'd like to know the whole plan." Ally smiled. "Is this about Gloria?"

"No." Charlotte narrowed her eyes. "Just trust me, Ally. It's a surprise."

"A surprise?" Ally smiled some. "A surprise that both you and Luke know about?" She shook her head. "You two are so sneaky. All you had to do was say, go spend the day with Luke, and I'd already be out the door."

"Great!" Charlotte laughed. "Then do that." She turned her toward the door. "He's already out there waiting for you."

Ally hugged her grandmother, then kissed Arnold and Peaches goodbye and headed out through the front door. As she'd been told, Luke waited for her at the end of the driveway.

"Ally, I know it's early." Luke smiled as he took her hand. "Don't worry, these errands won't take long."

"Oh, Mee-Maw told me that the two of you concocted some kind of plan." Ally rolled her eyes, then kissed him. "Whatever you two planned is fine with me, all I care about is getting to spend some time with you."

"Sounds perfect to me."

As Luke whirled her around town, stopping for breakfast, then a few groceries, then a visit to the library, Ally tried to figure out his plan.

"What is the point of all of this?" Ally laughed as he checked out a few books. "You didn't need me along for any of these errands."

"Need, no. Wanted, yes." Luke winked at her, then led her back out to the car. "Are you ready for lunch, yet?"

"Honestly Luke, can we just stop for a few minutes. Maybe we could go for a walk together?" Ally rubbed her hand over his. "I've missed you so much these past few days. I know we saw each other a bit and talked, but it's not the same as really being together. I'd rather just feel your hand in mine, and listen to you talk to me about anything."

"I'm sorry, I'm just a little nervous." Luke's cheeks reddened as he curled his fingers around her hand.

"Nervous?" Ally laughed. "What could you possibly have to be nervous about?" She kissed him, then met his eyes. "I can't wait to start planning the wedding again. When do you think we can do it? A month or so?"

"That's such a long time." Luke sighed as he wrapped his arms around her. "Do you think we have to wait that long?"

"It's going to take some time to get things rearranged." Ally scrunched up her nose. "Plus, we have to pick a new place to have it. Unless, we just forget about all of that and just get married. I don't need all of that, I just want to marry you."

"Me, too. But I think it would be nice to mark the special day." Luke raised an eyebrow. "Are you sure you haven't changed your mind about marrying me?"

"What are you talking about?" Ally smiled. "What did I just say? I can't wait to marry you."

"Great. Then we have one more stop to make." Luke opened the car door for her.

"Okay, but it better be something fun!" Ally settled in the passenger seat.

"I hope it will be." Luke drove back toward the cottage.

"Wait, why are we going this way? Do you have to go to work?"

"No, not going to work." Luke smiled, then patted her knee.

"What's this?" Ally stared at the collection of cars lined up along the road, then glanced over at Luke as he parked the car in front of the cottage.

"You can say no if you want to." Luke took her hands in his and looked into her eyes. "It might have been a ridiculous idea."

"What idea?" Ally frowned as she searched his eyes. "Luke, just tell me."

"I know that you said you would wait for the wedding, but to be honest with you, I couldn't wait." Luke's hands tightened around hers. "I was so looking forward to seeing you walk down the aisle, and hearing us announced as husband and wife. I know, I may not always have the time or the thoughtfulness to make it clear to you just how much I love you, Ally, and I thought this might be one way I could show you that."

Ally's eyes widened as she began to put the clues together. "Luke, what have you done?"

"Nothing." Luke took a sharp breath. "Absolutely

nothing, if you don't like the idea, I promise, all of it can be undone." He stepped out of the car, then walked around to the passenger side and opened her door. "I only want you to be happy."

"You always make me happy." Ally took his hand. "What's going on here?"

Ally looked toward the cottage door just as her grandmother stepped through it. She wore the sage-colored dress that she'd carefully selected for Ally's wedding. They had chosen it together.

As Ally turned back to Luke, he lowered to one knee and looked up into her eyes.

"Ally, will you marry me, today?" Luke stroked his thumb across the back of her hand. "Right here? Right now?"

"What?" Ally gasped. "You can't be serious!"

"I know it's not what we planned, and if you don't think it's a good idea, I understand. I just couldn't wait any longer, Ally. But I will, if that's what you want." Luke frowned as he gazed into her eyes.

Ally noticed the flowers scattered across the walkway that led around the side of the cottage. She heard voices coming from the backyard. As her heart pounded, music began to play.

Luke held her gaze, his cheeks flushed, and his

hand tight around hers. "Ally, are you going to answer me?"

"Didn't I?" Ally smiled as she stared into his eyes. "I could have sworn I shouted yes at least four times."

"Yes!" Luke laughed as he jumped back to his feet and swept her up into his arms.

"Luke!" Ally squealed as he carried her toward the door of the cottage. "You're supposed to do this after the wedding!"

"Like I said, I couldn't wait!" Luke laughed as he set her down in front of Charlotte. Jeff stood a few steps behind her. A wide smile on his lips.

"Don't worry, Ally, I have a makeup artist, hairdresser, your dress, I have everything you need." Charlotte waved her hand at Luke. "Now scoot, no seeing the bride before the wedding!"

"Of course!" Luke held up his hands as he backed away toward Jeff.

As Ally prepared for the wedding, surrounded by her grandmother, Mrs. Bing, Mrs. Cale, and Mrs. White, she felt as if she'd fallen right into a dream.

"But the food, and the cake." Ally's mind reeled. "How can everything be ready?"

"We took care of all of that, darling." Mrs. Bing smiled.

"The cake is ready." Charlotte smiled.

"Thank you all so much." Ally grinned at them, then took a peek through the back window. The backyard had been transformed with lace, flowers, and ribbons. An archway stood right at the entrance of the garden, flanked by several of her friends. She caught sight of Luke already in his suit as he paced back and forth. "He looks so nervous."

"As he should be." Charlotte turned Ally toward the mirror. "He's about to marry the most beautiful woman in Blue River!"

"Oh, Mee-Maw!" Ally rolled her eyes, then laughed. "I still can't believe this is happening."

"Would you have wanted it any other way?" Charlotte held her gaze. "We can still change things if you want."

"No, Mee-Maw, it's absolutely perfect." Ally wrapped her arm around her grandmother's. "I'm ready for you to walk me down the aisle."

"Wonderful, but we have to wait for the ring bearer and the flower pig." Charlotte laughed as she guided Ally to the back door, just as Arnold and Peaches bolted toward the archway.

Peaches had a tiny cushion strapped to her back. Arnold snorted his way through the piles of flower petals that led the way to the archway.

Ally couldn't stop laughing, until her eyes settled on Luke.

Luke turned to look at her, as all of their friends fell silent.

The look in his eyes, matched the lurch of her heart. She was filled with excitement, and awe. As she took her first step down the aisle, she yearned for the next, and the life that would unfold with Luke's hand in hers. Maybe things weren't as she planned, but there wasn't a single thing she would change. She was ready for their next adventure. She just hoped it didn't involve another dead body.

The End

MOCHA CAKE WITH MOCHA
BUTTERCREAM FROSTING RECIPE

Ingredients:

Cake

1 tablespoon instant coffee powder or granules

1/2 cup boiling water

2 sticks (1 cup) butter, at room temperature

1 cup brown sugar

1 cup granulated sugar

3 eggs, at room temperature

1 teaspoon vanilla extract

2 1/2 cups all-purpose flour

2/3 cup unsweetened cocoa powder

2 teaspoons baking powder

1 teaspoon baking soda

3/4 cup buttermilk, at room temperature

Mocha Buttercream Frosting

1 tablespoon instant coffee powder or granules

1/4 cup boiling water

2 sticks (1 cup) butter, at room temperature

1/8 cup unsweetened cocoa powder, sifted

3 to 4 cups superfine sugar, sifted

Semisweet chocolate for decorating (optional)

Preparation:

Preheat the oven to 350 degrees Fahrenheit.

Butter and line the base of 2 x 8-inch round cake pans.

Dissolve the instant coffee in the boiling water and leave aside to cool.

Beat the butter for about 2 minutes until smooth. Add the sugar and beat until light and fluffy.

Add the eggs one at a time beating between each addition.

Add the vanilla extract and prepared cooled coffee and mix until combined.

In another bowl sift together the flour, cocoa powder, baking powder and baking soda. Mix together.

Gradually add the dry ingredients alternating with the buttermilk to the egg and butter mixture.

Divide the batter between the prepared cake pans.

Bake in the pre-heated oven for about 26 to 32 minutes, until a skewer inserted into the middle comes out clean.

Leave the cakes to cool in the cake pans for about 10 minutes and then remove from the pans and cool on a wire rack. Once cooled remove the parchment paper from the base of the cakes.

To make the mocha buttercream frosting, dissolve the

instant coffee in the boiling water and leave aside to cool. Beat the butter for about 2 minutes until smooth. Mix in the cocoa powder and 3 cups of the superfine sugar. Gradually add the prepared cooled coffee, mixing between each addition. Add more superfine sugar if required to get the desired consistency.

Top one of the cakes with the frosting and place the other on top. Spread the frosting over the top and sides of the cake.

Grate or use a vegetable peeler to create curls of the semisweet chocolate and sprinkle over the top of the cake to decorate (optional).

Enjoy!!

ABOUT THE AUTHOR

Cindy Bell is a USA Today and Wall Street Journal Bestselling Author. She is the author of the Little Leaf Creek, Wagging Tail, Donut Truck, Dune House, Sage Gardens, Chocolate Centered, Macaron Patisserie, Nuts about Nuts, Bekki the Beautician, Heavenly Highland Inn and Wendy the Wedding Planner cozy mystery series.

Cindy has always loved reading, but it is only recently that she has discovered her passion for writing romantic cozy mysteries. She loves walking along the beach thinking of the next adventure her characters can embark on.

You can sign up for her newsletter so you are notified of her latest releases at http://www. cindybellbooks.com.

ALSO BY CINDY BELL

CHOCOLATE CENTERED COZY MYSTERIES

The Sweet Smell of Murder

A Deadly Delicious Delivery

A Bitter Sweet Murder

A Treacherous Tasty Trail

Pastry and Peril

Trouble and Treats

Fudge Films and Felonies

Custom-Made Murder

Skydiving, Soufflés and Sabotage

Christmas Chocolates and Crimes

Hot Chocolate and Homicide

Chocolate Caramels and Conmen

Picnics, Pies and Lies

Devils Food Cake and Drama

Cinnamon and a Corpse

Cherries, Berries and a Body

Christmas Cookies and Criminals

Jewelry Can Be Deadly

Numbers Can Be Deadly

Memories Can Be Deadly

Paintings Can Be Deadly

Snow Can Be Deadly

Tea Can Be Deadly

Greed Can Be Deadly

Clutter Can Be Deadly

DUNE HOUSE COZY MYSTERIES

Seaside Secrets

Boats and Bad Guys

Treasured History

Hidden Hideaways

Dodgy Dealings

Suspects and Surprises

Ruffled Feathers

A Fishy Discovery

Danger in the Depths

Celebrities and Chaos

Pups, Pilots and Peril

Tides, Trails and Trouble

Racing and Robberies

Athletes and Alibis

Manuscripts and Deadly Motives

Pelicans, Pier and Poison

Sand, Sea and a Skeleton

Pianos and Prison

Relaxation, Reunions and Revenge

A Tangled Murder

WAGGING TAIL COZY MYSTERIES

Murder at Pawprint Creek (prequel)

Murder at Pooch Park

Murder at the Pet Boutique

A Merry Murder at St. Bernard Cabins

Murder at the Dog Training Academy

Murder at Corgi Country Club

A Merry Murder on Ruff Road

Murder at Poodle Place

Murder at Hound Hill

Murder at Rover Meadows

DONUT TRUCK COZY MYSTERIES

Deadly Deals and Donuts

Fatal Festive Donuts

Bunny Donuts and a Body

Strawberry Donuts and Scandal

Frosted Donuts and Fatal Falls

Donut Holes and Homicide

NUTS ABOUT NUTS COZY MYSTERIES

A Tough Case to Crack

A Seed of Doubt

Roasted Peanuts and Peril

Chestnuts, Camping and Culprits

BEKKI THE BEAUTICIAN COZY MYSTERIES

Hairspray and Homicide

A Dyed Blonde and a Dead Body

Mascara and Murder

Pageant and Poison

Conditioner and a Corpse

Mistletoe, Makeup and Murder

Hairpin, Hair Dryer and Homicide

Blush, a Bride and a Body

Shampoo and a Stiff

Cosmetics, a Cruise and a Killer

Lipstick, a Long Iron and Lifeless

Camping, Concealer and Criminals

Treated and Dyed

A Wrinkle-Free Murder

A MACARON PATISSERIE COZY MYSTERY SERIES

Sifting for Suspects

Recipes and Revenge

Mansions, Macarons and Murder

HEAVENLY HIGHLAND INN COZY MYSTERIES

Murdering the Roses

Dead in the Daisies

Killing the Carnations

Drowning the Daffodils

Suffocating the Sunflowers

Books, Bullets and Blooms

A Deadly Serious Gardening Contest

A Bridal Bouquet and a Body

Digging for Dirt

WENDY THE WEDDING PLANNER COZY
MYSTERIES

Matrimony, Money and Murder

Chefs, Ceremonies and Crimes

Knives and Nuptials

Mice, Marriage and Murder